Tangled Up in Luck

MERRILL WYATT

TANGLED UP IN LUCK

WITHDRAWN

Margaret K. McElderry Books

New York London Toronto Sydney New Delhi

MARGARET K. McELDERRY BOOKS
An imprint of Simon & Schuster Children's Publishing Division
1230 Avenue of the Americas, New York, New York 10020

For information about special discounts for bulk purchases, please contact Simon & Schuster Special Sales at 1-866-506-1949 or business@simonandschuster.com.
The Simon & Schuster Speakers Bureau can bring authors to your live event. For more information or to book an event, contact the Simon & Schuster Speakers Bureau at 1-866-248-3049 or visit our website at www.simonspeakers.com.
Interior design by Rebecca Syracuse
The text for this book was set in Chronicle Display.
Manufactured in the United States of America
0921 FFG
First Edition
2 4 6 8 10 9 7 5 3 1
CIP data for this book is available from the Library of Congress.
Library of Congress Cataloging-in-Publication Data
Names: Wyatt, Merrill, author.
Title: Tangled up in luck / Merrill Wyatt.
Description: First edition. | New York : Margaret K. McElderry Books, [2021] | Audience: Ages 8–12. | Audience: Grades 4–6. | Summary: Seventh graders Sloane and Amelia are devastated to be paired for a research project about long-lost jewels, but soon they are finding clues hidden for nearly a century—and realize they are being used.
Identifiers: LCCN 2020052011 (print) | LCCN 2020052012 (ebook) | ISBN 9781534495791 (hardcover) | ISBN 9781534495807 (paperback) | ISBN 9781534495814 (ebook)
Subjects: CYAC: Middle schools—Fiction. | Schools—Fiction. | Friendship—Fiction. | Mystery and detective stories.
Classification: LCC PZ7.1.W975 Tan 2021 (print) | LCC PZ7.1.W975 (ebook) | DDC [Fic]—dc23
LC record available at https://lccn.loc.gov/2020052011
LC ebook record available at https://lccn.loc.gov/2020052012

For Sean and Abigail, and
the serendipity that brought
you both into my life

Tangled Up in Luck

Dear Reader,

Much like our two protagonists, you are about to embark on a mystery full of twists and turns. There will be both helpers and suspects—and it will frequently be difficult to tell who is who. A detective is only as good as their research materials, as our protagonists are about to find out. To prevent you from getting tangled up in this twisted mystery too, here is a guide to all you will encounter:

Sloane's Family—Present Day

Sloane Osburn..a thirteen-year-old seventh grader

David Osburn...Sloane's orthodontist dad

Maisy Osburn...Sloane's deceased mother

Granny Pearl...David's mother

Granny Kitty...Maisy's mother

Nanna Tia...Maisy's grandmother

Amelia's Family—Present Day

Amelia Miller-Poe..a twelve-year-old seventh grader

Amanda Miller...Amelia's financial-advisor mom

Alexander Poe...Amelia's father, the Judge

Aiden Poe...Amelia's half brother

Ashley Miller...Amelia's half sister

Miscellaneous Helpers (and Some Eventual Suspects)—Present Day

Mr. Roth..an English teacher

Principal Stuckey..................................principal of Wauseon Middle School

Belinda Gomez....................................a librarian at the Wauseon Public Library

Milton Unserios...museum curator at the
Fulton County Historical Society

Timothy Neikirk...a ninety-year-old auctioneer

Norma Cooke...a fashion designer for
concrete garden animals

The Hoäl Family—1855–1940

Jacob...orphan, circus owner, millionaire,
                                                    and onetime friend to Thomas Kerr

Lucretia...Jacob's wife

Charles...Jacob's son

Lucy...Charles's daughter

Charlotte..Charles's granddaughter

The Kerr Family—1855–1940

Thomas...clown, circus owner, carpenter,
                                                    and onetime friend to Jacob Hoäl

Beatrice..Thomas's wife

Oscar..Thomas's son

Johnny...Oscar's son

Prologue
School Projects Are Dangerous

Sloane Osburn dove behind a gravestone.

An acorn whizzed through the air where she'd been running only a fraction of a second before. Instead of smashing against her forehead, it chipped off a piece of another headstone. Granted, the slab was almost two hundred years old and fragile. But some of Sloane's body parts were fragile too, if not nearly as old.

No doubt another acorn had already been loaded into the slingshot, waiting for Sloane to scamper out from behind the stone. Like this was some sort of carnival game, with millions of dollars' worth of Victorian jewels as the prize for the winner.

"Sloane! Sloane!" her friend Amelia Miller-Poe called from the scrubby weeds on the other side of the cemetery. "Have you been hit, Sloane? Are you dying? It would be terribly tragic if we died together!"

As she huddled against the cold limestone, Sloane sighed in relief. If Amelia could talk dramatically about dying, then she was definitely okay. When Amelia stopped talking like that, you needed to worry.

"You're not dying, Amelia!" Sloane risked a peek around the edge of the stone.

She'd picked the wrong time to look. An acorn clipped her ear. Clapping a hand to the side of her head, Sloane jerked back behind the gravestone.

"She *might* be dying," the voice of their attacker called cheerfully. "You won't know unless you come out to see!"

"Don't do it!" Amelia cried woozily (but still dramatically). "I shall sacrifice myself nobly! Don't worry about me, Sloane! Save the long-lost Cursed Hoäl Treasure!"

The treasure. Amelia wasn't wrong about it being cursed. Who would have thought anyone else would really be looking for it over a hundred years later?

Who would have thought this whole school project was just a setup? To use the brains of middle-school kids to solve a riddle no adult had figured out in years: Whatever happened to the lost Hoäl jewels?

True, she and Amelia had figured it out. But a little too late.

Still, none of this would have happened if they hadn't been forced to work together. If Sloane and Amelia ended up stoned to death by acorns, it was going to be the school's fault for requiring group projects.

Bitterly, Sloane hoped everyone would be happy then. Why did teachers never listen to students when they said it was evil to force kids to work with people who weren't their friends?

Because this group project was definitely evil.

Or, at the very least, it had been organized by an evil person.

And that person wasn't going to stop until they got what they wanted.

1

An Unlucky Beginning

Exactly One Week Ago

It all began the Friday before, which should have been a lucky time of year. It was only two weeks until summer break. Plus, that was the day of the seventh grade's annual trip to Principal Stuckey's farm. The teachers called it "Outdoor Education" and enthused about all of the biodiversity and local history their students would be able to study. However, in reality, everyone knew it was just an excuse to get out of the classroom. Whether students or teachers, everyone was exhausted from all the spring testing required to prove they'd learned something that year. Outdoor Education was the reward for not dropping dead during it.

Speaking of dropping dead, that was exactly what Amelia Miller-Poe pretended to do after she accidentally tripped getting off the bus. Well, maybe accidentally. With Amelia, you never knew. It could have been on purpose.

Anyone else would have had the sense to creep away in humiliation. Or else play it up for laughs, if they were brave enough.

Not Amelia.

"I've fallen!" she gasped, clutching at her throat as she collapsed onto the ground. "I think I've broken my neck!"

Eyes closed, curly red hair spread out across the grass, she lay there as though dead. The other kids piled up on the school bus steps, unable to get out without stepping on her. They giggled nervously, trying to figure out what they should do.

Having already gotten off the bus, Sloane stood awkwardly off to the side. Her first instinct was to go help the girl. But if she did that, Amelia would probably attach herself to Sloane for the rest of the field trip. Then Sloane might as well join the girl on the ground and let all of the seventh grade laugh at them. Hanging out with Amelia was guaranteed social death.

"What's wrong with you people?" bellowed a girl with a big bow in her high ponytail as she elbowed her way to the bus door. Mackenzie "Mac Attack" Snyder, Sloane's volleyball teammate and friend. Spotting Amelia on the ground, her outrage turned to a sneer. "Oh. Em. Gee. Someone killed the yeti."

On the ground, Amelia quivered at the mention of the nickname. All of the other kids snickered as Mackenzie sprung from the bus step to jump over Amelia. She landed neatly on the other side and flounced off, snapping, "C'mon, Sloane!" The rest of the kids followed her lead, narrowly missing Amelia's legs with their sneakers. The bus driver yelled at them to stop and be careful, but no one listened.

Sloane didn't follow Mackenzie. Instead, she tugged at her own ponytail, hearing her mom whisper in her ear, "C'mon, Slayer Sloane. That could have been me when I was in seventh grade. If you can spike a ball to win the state volleyball tournament, you can give her a hand up." Of course, her mom wasn't *really* there.

Wouldn't be anywhere ever again. Yet Sloane knew her mom so well, she knew exactly what her mom would have said.

So, she dove forward and yanked Amelia up off the ground. "Would you just stop? Don't act weird today, and maybe people will actually quit calling you a yeti!"

Her words came out way more harshly than Sloane had intended. In her mind, she could feel her imaginary mom wince. Sloane really had wanted to be kind. But when she got stressed, she also became pretty intense.

Amelia pulled herself free. Unlike all of the other kids in their jeans and hoodies, she wore a jean jacket and white satin dress that had to be somebody's old communion dress or flower girl costume. "It doesn't matter what I do. No one here is ever going to call *me* a slayer."

With that, Amelia marched off. Sloane watched her go, feeling a combination of relief, frustration, and guilt.

Lots and lots of guilt, actually.

Sloane tugged again at her ponytail. Unlike Mackenzie, she didn't keep a bow in hers. Also, unlike Mackenzie, Sloane spent a lot of time worrying that people might be able to read her mind.

Everyone thought she was scary-focused. And Sloane was.

But only because she was constantly on alert, afraid the other kids would finally figure out what a nerd she really was. Not the good kind of nerd, either. An Amelia kind of nerd.

Not today, however. No, today was all about relaxing. Every year, Principal Stuckey let the classes explore the woods, streams, and meadows of her farm. The students would collect samples of leaves and bugs. Then they'd learn about the first European settlers arriving in the area and the Native Americans who had been minding their own business and having a perfectly lovely time up until then.

That was what their teachers had planned, at least. None of the students cared too much about what they learned as they roamed over the new spring grass and under the freshly budding trees. Everyone just savored the fact that the spring weather had *finally* arrived, over a month late. That the rules and structure of school were tossed aside like the last of the winter's snow. While they collected flora and fauna samples and—

"AUGH! A bee! I've been stung by a bee!" Once more, Amelia collapsed to the ground. "I might be allergic! I could be dying! I feel my throat swelling—"

Before Amelia could continue, one of Sloane's other teammates/friends named Mylie held up a stick. "It was just this poking your ankle."

Crossing her arms, Amelia scowled and harrumphed. She clearly liked her explanation better. Because a little while later . . .

"Look! It's deadly nightshade! And I've touched it! I'm dying!"

This time it was their science teacher, Mrs. Lemons, who explained that no, that was a purple violet; deadly nightshade didn't grow around here—you couldn't die just from touching it, and violets looked nothing like nightshade anyhow.

"No one has any imagination," Amelia complained.

"No one has a *yeti's* imagination." Mylie's best friend, Kylee, laughed, looking to Mackenzie for approval.

When Mac laughed too, everyone except for Sloane joined in as well. Sloane's imaginary mom crossed her arms in disapproval at the other kids.

Amelia went as bright red as her hair and stomped off.

Sloane again tugged anxiously at her ponytail. Realizing it, she yanked her hand away and stuck her nose up in the air. Maybe if she acted bored, everyone would follow her lead and pretend to be bored too.

Maybe if she acted bored *enough,* everyone would stop calling Amelia a yeti.

Maybe it would be like Sloane had never come up with the name for her in the first place. In her mind, Sloane's mom gave her a hug. Sloane touched her own arm, wishing she could feel it for real.

The whole class hiked their way over fallen logs and through tangled vines to reach the middle of Principal Stuckey's woods. A swampy stream flowed sluggishly between the trees. Wearing a pair of leather waders, Mrs. Lemons stood in the chilly water, waiting to show them some crayfish she'd caught. However, as she opened her mouth to begin the lesson, Amelia spoke up.

"This would be the perfect setting for a murder mystery," she observed breathlessly. Clasping her hands together, she looked out over the glassy sheet of water with shining eyes. "Imagine a body drifting up against Mrs. Lemons's leg like some kind of shark. Well, like a dead shark, anyhow."

Mrs. Lemons's eyes bugged out quite a bit. In spite of herself, she glanced nervously over her shoulder. Whether looking for a shark, a body, or some horrifying combination of the two, Sloane didn't know.

Everyone else gaped at Amelia. And mumbled about crazy yetis. Sloane kept tugging at her ponytail until Mrs. Lemons collected herself and began the lesson on water purification. Mylie helped Kylee, and Mackenzie helped Sloane, but Amelia worked all by herself to study the murky water in the mason jars.

By the time they finished, everyone had wet shoes and cold hands. For the next activity, Sloane and Amelia's group moved to the edge of the woods to join their English teacher, Mr. Roth, for whatever easy-as-cake assignment he was going to give them about the farm.

Little did they know it, but *this* assignment was about to become more trouble than a whole nest of bees, an entire forest of hemlock, and a dead shark combined.

(It would, admittedly, be slightly less trouble than being in the water with a living shark.)

Mr. Roth met them in a small, forgotten cemetery surrounded by a rusting iron fence. It must have once been out in the open fields, but these days it was half swallowed up by old trees.

They walked under an iron archway that said SAUGLING CEMETERY. Sloane wondered who the Sauglings were and how long ago they had lived here. There were little cemeteries like this tucked away all over northwest Ohio, her great-granny

Nanna Tia had told Sloane and her mom. Nanna Tia said that a hundred and fifty years ago, a lot of the farm families had their own cemeteries rather than using the ones in the towns.

Which was both kinda creepy and exactly the sort of nerdy comment Sloane had enough sense to keep to herself.

Unlike Amelia.

"There are places like this all over," Amelia announced to no one in particular as they all tried to find places to stand among the weeds and crooked stones. "People used to do that, you know. Have family cemeteries. Kind of like how some people still bury their pets in the backyard."

Mackenzie, Kylee, and Mylie all gaped at Amelia in unflattering disbelief. Sloane resisted the urge to cover her face with her hands and did her best to look bored.

"Er, she's right, actually." Mr. Roth cleared his throat sheepishly, surprising everyone else. Next to him, Amelia smiled smugly.

Their teacher beckoned everyone toward a particularly large stone plinth. It had the name HOÄL chiseled into it, though the letters were half worn away by the years of wind, sun, and ice. One side also said JACOB, 1850–1887 while the other side read LUCRETIA, 1855–1887. Nearby, there was a stone with a fat baby on it. Sloane was pretty sure it was supposed to be a cherub, but time and the weather had worn away the wings. The faded letters on it read LUCKY, which seemed like a very bad joke to Sloane.

"We're here in this graveyard so I can tell you a particularly tragic tale. It's a story full of woe, mystery, death—and even explosions and missing treasure." Mr. Roth assumed his storyteller tone.

Between the branches overhead and the clouds gathered around the sun, the temperature seemed to drop twenty degrees. Sloane shivered, hunching her shoulders and pulling the sleeves of her hoodie down over her hands.

A breeze stirred last autumn's leaves, dead at their feet. Sloane crunched an acorn with her toe, not at all sure she was going to like this story.

"It concerns the old Hoäl house out at the end of Burr Road." That was a big, ancient rambling mansion that someone had bought a few years ago and turned into a day spa and luxury bed-and-breakfast. It still looked creepily haunted to Sloane, but it was the sort of place adults drooled over.

Sloane's dad had taken her mom there as a treat right after she was diagnosed with cancer. Back when everyone thought she'd get well again.

Mr. Roth continued, "It was built in 1887 by Jacob Hoäl, a self-made millionaire. Jacob was an orphan who was adopted by a farm family. He was the son of German immigrants, the Hoäls— that's *H, A, O, L*, pronounced like 'hall.' They died soon after they arrived in Wauseon, and he was taken in by the Zimmerman family. But in those days, people didn't adopt kids to love them and take care of them. The Zimmermans adopted Jacob so they could have someone to work for free on their farm. Jacob worked hard and was never paid for any of it. So, one day when they were just a little older than you guys, Jacob and the farmer's son, Thomas, ran away to join the circus."

Ugh. Circuses. Sloane wasn't a fan. Though she supposed hanging out with creepy clowns was better than working for free for people who were mean to you. Either way, definitely not lucky.

"He became a millionaire by joining the circus?" Mackenzie interrupted skeptically. Of all of the seventh graders, Sloane suspected that Mac Attack Snyder was the most likely to someday become an actual millionaire. She was probably looking for tips.

"He worked his way up through the ranks and ended up owning it—only to sell the circus to his friend Thomas and then invest the money in the stock market." Mr. Roth cocked an eyebrow mysteriously. *"That* made him a millionaire. A multimillionaire, actually. Then he returned to Wauseon with his wife and baby son to build a mansion at the edge of town. But his good fortune didn't last long. The house hadn't even been finished when Jacob and Lucretia died tragically in a train crash."

Jacob and Lucretia Hoäl. The names on the tall marble plinth in front of them.

Sloane scrunched up her shoulders. She didn't want to hear about people dying tragically. There was nothing lucky about it, no matter what the stone next to her said.

"If anyone has been inside the old Hoäl mansion, you'll know that it's full of complicated wooden carvings and marble floors. In his study, Jacob even had the workmen add a secret safe behind a wood panel. Right before the family left on their last trip, Lucretia stored all of her valuable jewelry in there, including a diamond necklace, emerald earrings, and a ruby tiara that once belonged to a czarina of Russia. Altogether, everything was valued at almost five hundred thousand dollars at that time. It would be worth even more than that now. In fact, thirteen million dollars more today."

That got the attention of even the kids who'd been secretly flicking acorn caps at each other. Including Sloane's friends Kylee and Mylie. They were even more impressed by Mr. Roth's next words.

"Yes, they were worth quite a bit of money. Enough to tempt Jacob's old friend Thomas into using dynamite to blow open the safe."

"Cool!" Mylie and Kylee breathed together. Several other students nodded in agreement.

"The theft was discovered early the next morning when workmen arrived to put the finishing touches on the mansion. A message was sent to Jacob and Lucretia in Chicago. They immediately hopped on the first train back to Wauseon, desperate to recover their lost jewels."

"Did they find them?" Amelia asked, grabbing Mr. Roth's arm and tugging like she could pump the answer out of him. "Did they find them? *Tell* me they found them!"

"They did not." Mr. Roth pried his arm free. "Lucretia's jewelry was worth so much that the robbery was big news all over the Midwest. Newspapers and police departments sent telegrams back and forth between each other through the railroad's telegraph system. So many telegrams, in fact, that someone at the railroad became distracted. Two trains were allowed onto the same track in Indiana. As a result, the Hoäl's eastbound train smashed into a westbound train, killing many people on both trains. Jacob and Lucretia Hoäl were among the dead—and so was Thomas himself. For, by a twist of fate, *he* was on that westbound train."

Sloane looked again at the names on the marble plinth. Those people had been smashed to smithereens. Because of the actions of a guy who probably used to be a clown. And all because they had the bad luck to get on the wrong train at the wrong time.

"And the baby?" Sloane couldn't help but ask, thinking about her own mother.

"Ah, the baby." Mr. Roth scratched at his chin to build up suspense. When the pause had lasted long enough to hook the attention of even those kids who were trying to act like they didn't care about some dumb baby, he added, "The baby did *not*, in fact . . . die." A relieved sigh swept through the cemetery before their teacher added, "But he was left an orphan. Just like his father had been."

Sloane knew she hated this story.

"Meanwhile, Lucretia's jewels were never seen again. The police searched the wreckage but found nothing. It was assumed Thomas must have given the jewels to someone, if he hadn't taken them onto the train. But if so, who? Whoever it was never tried to sell them. Every jeweler in the country was looking for them. Eventually, people decided the jewels must be hidden in town somewhere. For a long time, they dredged wells and dug up gardens, but not so much as a single gemstone has been seen since. Which doesn't make for a very good story, does it? Stories need a conclusion—and so all of you are going to provide one. Working with a partner, you will have until one week from Monday to research this cold case and decide what *you* think happened to the jewels."

"That's easy." Mackenzie waved her hand dismissively, bow bobbing as she tossed her head. "We'll just look it up online."

"Ah! Ha-ha!" Mr. Roth did a happy dance and then seemed to realize that he was literally dancing on someone's grave. Immediately, he stopped and said more somberly, "You are welcome to look it up online, Mackenzie. But you'll soon discover that there's very little information about it. This all happened long before the invention of the computer, let alone the internet or Google. This assignment will require you and your partner to work together to find old newspaper articles at the library, research the archives at the Fulton County Historical Society, and even speak with an old-timer or two."

Ugh. It was *May* and here Mr. Roth was giving them *work*! There had to be some sort of law against that. What was even the point of learning stuff they weren't going to be tested on?

Everyone except for Amelia tried to catch someone else's eye. It was like a silent game of musical chairs, with no one wanting to be left unpartnered at the end of it. Thus being forced by Mr. Roth to work with Amelia. Who wasn't even bothering to try to find a partner. Instead, she had her hands clasped together, a dreamy look on her face. No doubt she was hoping to work by herself and present some sort of bizarre video or—Sloane didn't know.

Maybe an interpretive dance.

Then Mr. Roth cheerfully announced, "Oh, and before you start choosing partners, you're going to draw Scrabble tiles out of a bag. Whoever has the same letter as you will be your partner."

"*What?*"

"But that's not fair!"

"Mr. Roth, you can't do that to us!"

The groans over having to do actual work so late in the year turned mutinous as everyone realized they might be stuck working with someone they hated. Sloane had to hand it to Mr. Roth for his bravery, making an announcement like that in a graveyard.

Where there were plenty of places to hide his body.

"It's important that you learn to cooperate with everyone, not just your friends," Mr. Roth informed them calmly, not at all threatened by the scowling and grumbling. "You're almost eighth graders, guys!"

So what? All of the eighth graders Sloane knew liked to work with their friends too.

Mr. Roth brought around a cloth bag filled with the Scrabble tiles. He also recorded who drew what letter as they took them out of the bag to make sure no one could secretly swap. Which, of course, was exactly what everyone had planned on doing until then.

When it was her turn, Sloane drew the letter *W*, which no one else had gotten so far. Mackenzie drew the letter *T*, which matched her up with Drake Weber, who she couldn't stand. Mylie and Kylee both managed to draw the letter *B*, so at least *they* got to work together.

One by one, the other kids were matched up too, while Amelia skulked about among the gravestones, trying to avoid being seen. She seemed to be operating on the theory that Mr. Roth might forget about her, thus allowing her to avoid partner work. She was short enough that it might actually work, if not for that bush of fiery hair.

As the number of kids left dwindled and still no one had pulled out a *W*, Sloane's heart first started to race and then slowed down in horror until it was practically dead. Instinctively, her fingers found her ponytail to twist it round and round.

Aside from Amelia, there were six kids left.

Come on, someone draw a W, Sloane thought.

Four kids left.

No, no, no, no, no . . .

Two kids.

Please.

No kids left.

"Let's see . . ." Mr. Roth checked his list and then looked up to pin Amelia against a tombstone with his gaze. She actually had her arms spread out, fingers splayed as her eyes darted about, looking for an escape route. Like their teacher was the warden and she an escaped prisoner he'd just turned the search light on.

He held up the remaining letter. A *W* to match the one in Sloane's sweating palm. "Amelia! It looks like you and Sloane are partners!"

Of all the luck.

2

ZEMBLANITY VS. SERENDIPITY

Though no one in the class knew it right then and there, it was no accident that Mr. Roth had assigned them this project. Someone had been talking to Mr. Roth, and that person had been filling his head with ideas.

Someone had stumbled across the forgotten fact that the jewels existed. That same someone wanted very badly to find them.

Thirteen million dollars can motivate some people to do all sorts of dreadful things.

Therefore, it was neither serendipity nor zemblanity that caused Mr. Roth to give the class such a terrible project.

The word "serendipity" means "fortunate good chance." It's sort of like being lucky times a billion. It's lucky to have a substitute show up instead of the regular, cranky teacher. It's serendipity if that means you get an extra day to finish the project you forgot was due that day, saving you from a zero and giving you enough time to get a respectable B minus. (Which was exactly how Amelia had managed to save her social studies grade earlier in the year.)

The opposite of serendipity is called zemblanity. It's not an official word yet, but rather one that was recently made up by the author William Boyd to describe Tyrannosaurus rex–sized bad luck.

Regular bad luck is forgetting that you had a project due. Zemblanity isn't just forgetting that project. Instead, zemblanity is losing your backpack with all of the notes that might have helped you throw something together at the last minute. Losing it because it fell out of the school bus window. All because you stood up to make room for the kid next to you to sit down. Just as the bus lurched forward before you expected it. Knocking you to the side. And tipping your backpack out the window, onto the road.

Where it bounced into a drainage ditch. That was full because it had been pouring all week long.

That's zemblanity.

(And that example had happened to Sloane in third grade.)

Most people have more experience with zemblanity than serendipity.

Sloane's problems with Amelia had started with a zemblanitatious encounter a month ago in April. Right before spring break, Sloane ran into Amelia by the checkout desk of the Wauseon Public Library on a snowy day.

(The fact that it was snowing in April was bad luck. Pretty much everything else that happened afterward was definitely *beyond* bad luck.)

On that almost-spring-break day, Sloane had a copy of a *Doctor Who* retrospective in her hands and was desperately hoping no one saw Slayer Sloane with something so nerdy. Seventh grade had been so much better than sixth grade. She'd spent that year in a gray haze of misery, which had descended after her mother's death from cancer. That was the year she'd been the Girl Whose Mom Just Died, a name that kids and teachers whispered behind their hands while throwing her pitying looks.

Now in seventh grade, she was Slayer Sloane, the Volleyball Queen. And even if she wasn't *entirely* certain who exactly that was, Sloane was positive that someone called a slayer didn't geek out on British science fiction.

But Sloane's mom had, and it had been their Saturday-night routine for as long as Sloane could remember: pizza and Doritos and the show her mom had loved as a child. They'd eat their junk food together on the couch while her dad jokingly protested that he'd like to watch something—anything—better. Yet he'd always end up watching it with them, even if he pretended like he didn't want to.

These days, it was just Sloane and her dad sitting on that couch. And he didn't make jokes anymore.

Who'd have thought you could miss corny dad jokes?

When Sloane saw the *Doctor Who* book on the library shelf, her heart warmed with the memory of those long-ago nights when they'd all sat together, eating greasy, salty food and getting lost in a world where it felt like anything could happen. Sloane's fingers reached out and snagged the book before she even knew what they were doing.

Then she heard Mackenzie's snide laughter on the other side of the library and panicked, stuffing the book under her hoodie like a thief.

That was still bad luck.

Mackenzie "Mac Attack" Snyder was with Mylie and Kylee. They hadn't spotted Sloane, but she had to get out of the library before they did. With her back turned to them and the book still hidden, she hurried toward the exit.

She wasn't really going to steal a library book. Just hide it until she got to the checkout desk.

Except that as Sloane rounded the corner, she smacked into Amelia Miller-Poe.

Literally.

Amelia had been turning the corner too, only from the opposite direction. Springy red hair haloed a stack of books so tall that they completely covered Amelia's face. Anyone else would have had the sense to put half of them down, but not Amelia.

WHOMP! Sloane barely had time to register what was happening, let alone react. They hit each other, and books went flying onto the floor. Along with both girls.

That was more than bad luck but not quite zemblanity.

The zemblanity kicked in when Sloane looked up to see Mackenzie, Mylie, and Kylee staring down at her.

And she realized the *Doctor Who* book had slid out of her hoodie to join the others on the floor.

Click went Mackenzie's phone, possibly taking a shot of Amelia surrounded by a mass of hair and books.

Or possibly taking a picture of Sloane with her nerd guide.

Amelia got up first, while Sloane closed her eyes and just lay there, thinking, *Yup. That's it. My social life is over. Well, it was nice while it lasted.*

Maybe if she lay here long enough with her eyes closed, something would distract everyone. Like—possibly—hopefully, a tornado. Or an earthquake. Or an alien invasion.

Any of those could happen. If she just lay there long enough.

"You look like a dead person," Amelia whispered in that breathy, dramatic voice of hers. "You aren't dead, are you, Sloane? I haven't murdered you, have I?"

There was something in Amelia's voice that implied that, while she'd be very sorry to have killed Sloane, she'd find it pretty interesting too.

Mackenzie's giggle yanked Sloane's eyes open.

"No, I'm not dead!" Sloane snapped. A shiver rippled all through her body, chasing away the happy memory she'd been holding on to of her mom, replacing it instead with a far less happy one of a casket and too many flowers and an aching emptiness that was so big and gray that Sloane had thought she'd never find her way to the other side of it. "Why would you even say that?"

"Oh." Amelia blinked several times. "I'm sorry. I didn't think about your mom dying. But, I mean, at least she wasn't murdered."

Sloane gaped at the other girl, her stomach knotting with so many emotions that she didn't think she'd ever be able to untangle it again.

Behind Amelia, Mackenzie at least stopped giggling. Instead, she and the other girls looked awkwardly away as Sloane transformed from Slayer Sloane back into the Girl Whose Mom Just Died.

Like Amelia was a thief who had snatched away Sloane's new identity, leaving her with the old, sad one instead.

In that moment, Sloane hated the other girl for it.

"We went to the funeral home," Amelia babbled, scrabbling around to pick up her books. Getting to her knees, Sloane frantically helped her, wanting Amelia gone as quickly as possible. "I'd never seen a dead person before."

Sloane dropped the book she had picked up like someone had set it on fire. "Would you please just stop talking?"

"I—I—I . . ." Amelia stammered, blushing so furiously that between her hair and freckles, she became a solid mass of embarrassment.

"Gawd," Mackenzie drawled, rolling her eyes. "Don't you know how to act around, like, other human beings?"

Rather than replying, Amelia hugged as many of her books as she could. She looked from girl to girl, mouth opening and shutting like a fish.

But rather than saying anything, she turned and fled.

Sloane sort of wished she'd thought to do that herself.

Kylee picked up the *Doctor Who* book from the floor and called after Amelia, "Hey, you forgot one of your books!"

But if Amelia had heard, she wasn't returning for anything.

"It's so *weird*," Mackenzie said with a laugh, taking the book from Kylee and flipping it open like she'd discovered Amelia's secret diary. "I mean, who's even into stuff like this?"

Of course, the answer was: lots of people. One of Sloane's cousins who lived down in Columbus was even in a *Doctor Who* club at his middle school. But this was Wauseon, Ohio. Population 6,500, deep in the farmlands in the northwest corner of Ohio.

People here were nice enough, but they didn't do different

hobbies and interests very well. They did sports and farming and that was about it. If anyone else in her class liked nerdy British science fiction, they had enough sense to keep it a deep, dark secret and join the basketball team or the 4-H club instead.

"I mean," Mackenzie said again, laughing harder as she pointed at a furry beast, "what even *is* that?"

"A yeti." The words slipped out before Sloane even realized she'd said them. That creeping gray gloom had wrapped itself around her heart, squeezing it tight. And it was all Amelia's fault. Annoying, annoying Amelia who just *had* to talk about death and funerals. Sloane hated her all the more. "That's a yeti. Which must be why she was checking out that book. She's looking at her family members."

The other girls looked at Sloane in confusion.

"Because she's so hairy." To her horror, Sloane could feel tears forming in her eyes. "She's like a yeti herself. A hairy, weird, dramatic yeti. Amelia the Yeti."

Mackenzie pulled up the picture she'd taken of Amelia on her phone. "That's hilarious! I've got to text that to the other girls on the team."

Mylie and Kylee laughed dutifully. Whether they really thought it was funny too, who knew? It was enough that the Mac Attack did. Off went their messages too.

Amelia the Yeti was born.

Maybe she should have felt bad. But for a moment, Sloane felt like she'd finally gotten a little bit even with all of the hurt the universe had sent her way.

By that evening, however, Sloane *did* feel bad. Her phone kept pinging with yeti jokes as the other girls on the volleyball team turned the picture of Amelia into a meme with all sorts of dumb comments around it. Then a kid named Schroeder joined in, and that set off the kids on the track team. Curled up in a fleece blanket with a pint of ice cream in her hands, Sloane finally turned her phone off.

She wished she'd never opened her mouth. Yeah, Amelia had really upset her with all of her talk about dead bodies and dead moms, but Sloane bet the other girl had just been nervous. No doubt, she had felt as embarrassed as Sloane had at making a fool of herself in front of Mackenzie, Kylee, and Mylie. Still, at least everyone would forget all about it in a day or two.

Except, they didn't.

Instead, the Yeti went viral. Or at least it did among the seventh graders at Wauseon Middle School. By the second day, no one even remembered that Sloane was the one who had come up with the name.

It was as if Amelia had always been the Yeti.

3

THROWN OUT OF A LIBRARY BY A BIKER

Amelia had never heard of either serendipity or zemblanity. She was also completely unaware that someone was setting her up along with the other seventh graders. She had no idea at all that they were being used to do all the hard work of discovering where, exactly, the Hoäl jewels were hidden.

Right now, Amelia had bigger problems than that.

Because it was Friday night, and that meant golf. And listening to her family talk at her. Not *to* her. At her.

"I see on PowerSchool that your English grade has dropped down to a C minus," her mom announced, as she whacked a golf ball over a rolling green hill at Ironwood Golf Club. She didn't say it cruelly or angrily, just factually. And briskly. Amanda Poe, financial advisor, said everything briskly.

"Don't you have Mr. Roth?" Amelia's half brother, Aiden Miller, barked before Amelia could answer. He teed up a ball and then whacked it over the same green hill. Like his stepmom, he didn't intend to be mean. It was just that everyone in their family said everything in too-loud, too-confident voices. Aiden was a sophomore at the University of Toledo, and he'd just moved back home that day for the summer break. "He's, like, the best teacher ever. How are you getting a C minus in his class?"

Amelia opened her mouth to answer, but her dad got in first as they all moved on to the next hole, chasing the balls like they were very slow golden retrievers. The Honorable Alexander Poe announced his verdict as though he was still sitting in his courtroom at the Fulton County Courthouse. Everyone always called him the Judge—even his own family. "She needs to apply herself more. Don't you, Amelia?"

Once again, Amelia tried to answer, but her half sister Ashley Poe, a student at UT as well, cut in first. "What you need is to be better organized, Amelia. I can help you put together a color-coded study system like I use."

"Yes, that's an excellent plan," their mom confirmed decisively.

"Listen to Ashley. She's a valuable resource." The Judge nodded enthusiastically. "She's never gotten so much as an A minus in her entire life, you know."

Amelia did know. It came up frequently.

"Aiden, either," her mom agreed.

Amelia knew that, too.

"You'll have to step up your game, Amelia." Her dad was trying to tease her as they reached the water hazard her ball had ended up in. Gloomily, she teed up her new ball as he continued, "Your siblings have left some big boots for you to fill!"

Fill with what, exactly? No one ever actually said. Personally, Amelia was voting for slugs.

Not that she didn't like her siblings. She did.

Well, sort of. Most of the time.

It was just that they were both so much older than her. And smarter than her. And more accomplished than her. And better looking than her. And, well, *everything* than her.

"We'll sign you up for summer lessons at Kumon," her mom declared.

"And put together a summer reading list of classic novels," her dad added.

"I'll organize your room and study desk," said Ashley.

"And I'll help you put together a summer workout routine," Aiden said. "An organized body leads to an organized mind."

Well, didn't that all sound perfectly awful?

Amelia's second ball ended up in the water hazard too. Her family had lots of advice on how to keep that from happening again.

The sun was setting by the time the game was over and they finally trudged back home to their enormous, sparkling house right on the golf course. Everything in the Miller-Poe house sparkled blandly, daring you to impress any sort of personality on it. Growing up, Amelia had never once been brave enough to make a pillow fort out of any of the couch cushions or play the-floor-is-hot-lava in the living room.

Even her bedroom sparkled. The pictures and furniture and *everything* had been picked out by an interior designer. Any time Amelia tried to alter any of it, the cleaners put things back exactly the way the designer had left them.

The only thing she had any control over was her clothes— and only then because everyone else left the house before she did in the morning and came back long after she'd arrived home in the afternoon. When they were around, they spent all of their time telling Amelia what to do.

The only place she could be herself was at school.

Where everyone let her know that being herself was the worst possible thing she could be. No one—not one single person—wanted to be her friend. That night, as Amelia slipped into a bed so perfect that it seemed to sneer at her, challenging her to get a single crease in the sheets, she couldn't help but think wistfully of how amazing it would be to have a friend. Just one person in all the world who liked her as she was, rather than wanting to change her or call her names.

One person who wouldn't think of her as the Yeti.

In a movie, that person would be Sloane Osburn. They'd start working together on Mr. Roth's project, only to discover how much they had in common. It would turn out that Sloane liked old black-and-white movies too! She'd reveal that she really hated volleyball but loved to dress up in costumes just like Amelia did! Sloane would listen to Amelia's ideas for the project, and rather than bossing her around, Sloane would think they were brilliant.

For one tiny moment, a bit of hope flared up inside of Amelia. It seemed to warm up even the cold, sparkling bedroom.

Then she remembered how Sloane had snapped at her after she fell off the bus. "Don't act weird today," the other girl had spit. The memory of it made her go all hot, but not in a cozy sort of way. In a lonely, ashamed sort of way.

It was just her luck to get stuck with Miss Perfect, Slayer Sloane Osburn. Who couldn't possibly ever be her friend. She sneered at Amelia like she was a slug ever since Amelia had bumped into her in the library last month and then blathered on about Sloane's dead mom. The memory of it was still enough to make Amelia cringe and pull the bedcovers up over her head in an attempt to hide from it.

True, Sloane never called her a yeti, and sometimes she'd even be sorta helpful. Like when she'd pulled Amelia up off the ground. But she always did it in a super annoyed sort of way. Worse, there was no chance she was going to listen to Amelia's ideas about this project, let alone think they were brilliant.

And Amelia had a *lot* of ideas for the project.

She'd been trying to start up a YouTube channel featuring 1920s-style black-and-white movies she'd made. However, so far, the only person who'd liked a single video Amelia had made was her grandma Suzy. Who was the one who'd gotten Amelia interested in old, silent movies in the first place.

If she made a movie for her project, she'd be able to upload it to both her YouTube channel *and* get an A on Mr. Roth's project, maybe getting her family off her back, too. The famous story of the missing Hoäl treasure *had* to generate view and likes. There were rich people! Stolen jewels! Tragic deaths in need of avenging!

Except that Sloane would no doubt want to make the same boring slideshow that everyone else was going to make.

Fortunately, Amelia didn't actually have to work with Sloane until Monday. That was when Belinda Gomez, the children's and young adult librarian from the Wauseon Public Library, was going to come into their English class with materials for them to use in their research. That gave Amelia an entire weekend to start her much-better project before she had to deal with whatever disaster Sloane wanted to put together.

Feeling just a bit better, Amelia dared to press her head against her bed pillow. It only dented a little—like it disapproved of her wrinkling things every bit as much as the cleaners did— but it was enough to allow Amelia to sleep, where she dreamed about a family who didn't boss her around and friends who actually accepted her at school. Which was lovely until she woke up Saturday morning to her big, sparkling room and reality.

Then she sort of wished she hadn't dreamed it at all. Thinking you had people who cared about you, only to discover that you didn't, was worse than never having anyone at all.

Shaking this off with determination, Amelia slid out of bed. Who cared about anyone else? Amelia knew she was brilliant even if no one else had figured it out yet. She rooted through the back of her walk-in closet for her secret stash of interesting clothing from the Goodwill store. She resurfaced with a long, swingy tweed coat and a hat that kinda-sorta looked like something Sherlock Holmes might wear.

If he was desperate.

Still, Amelia was perfectly happy to be any sort of a Sherlock Holmes, even a desperate one. She swung the coat around her shoulders and settled the cap on her head. Then she tucked an enormous, slightly cracked magnifying glass into her belt before checking herself out in the mirror.

She looked *exactly* like Sherlock Holmes.

Well, more or less.

If Sherlock Holmes had outfitted himself from what he could find at the Goodwill store.

And if he had freckles and too much springy red hair.

And he was short.

And a girl.

But other than that, the resemblance was *spot-on*.

Everyone else had already gotten up early to either go jogging or work out or whatever other terrible things they did for fun. Fortunately, Aiden had just gotten back from his run and was drinking a protein shake when Amelia went downstairs to make herself a couple of peanut-butter-and-pickle sandwiches for breakfast. He blinked at her strange appearance but was chugging his shake and unable to talk.

"Can you give me a ride to the library, please?" she asked as she slapped her sandwiches together. "I want to get right to work on my project. Like you guys said."

She wasn't at all sure that they'd said that, but Miller-Poes always took credit for good ideas.

"Sure. Are you doing some sort of skit?" he asked, giving her clothes the side-eye as he grabbed his keys. They went out into the family's massive five-car garage. Not surprisingly, it sparkled with cleanliness and lack of personality.

"Something like that."

Aiden spent the entire five-minute drive telling her exactly how she should do her skit. Amelia leaned her face as far as she could out the open car window and tried to ignore him as much as possible.

Her brother dropped her off in front of the old redbrick library building before hurrying to his summer job overseeing the other lifeguards at the public pool. Elm Street was pretty much empty since most people weren't out of bed yet. Unless they were at the baseball diamonds a mile down the street, or the soccer fields outside of town.

As soon as her brother peeled away, Amelia pulled a selfie stick out from beneath her heavy tweed coat. She snapped her phone into it and announced in a dramatic whisper, "And so begins the investigation into the Mysterious Case of the Missing Jewels."

She wasn't planning on using sound, but just in case she changed her mind later, Amelia felt it was best to say everything as theatrically as possible.

"What. Are. You. Wearing?" a familiar voice behind her asked in disbelief.

Amelia couldn't quite believe what was happening either. In a state of shock, she flipped off her camera and slowly turned around.

Slayer Sloane stood a few feet down the sidewalk, a notebook clutched to her chest and her lip curled distastefully. She stood between two elderly women wearing brightly colored floral tracksuits, gold fanny packs, and immaculate white running shoes.

"Sloane-y! That's no way to greet a friend!" one chided gently and then pinched Sloane's cheek. Amelia assumed she was probably Sloane's grandma, since grandmas everywhere had pretty much cornered the market on cheek-pinching.

"Are you here to do research too?" the other woman asked Amelia cheerfully.

"Er." Amelia tucked her selfie stick back under her coat and tried to think of something to say. She wasn't Sloane's friend. She wasn't anyone's friend. And what was Sloane doing here? Didn't she have softball practice or cool people to be hanging out with or something—*anything*—else to do? "Um. Yes?"

"So is our Sloane-y!" The first grandma couldn't have looked more delighted by this.

Sloane couldn't have looked more appalled by this.

"Well, you two have fun!" The second grandma pinched Sloane's cheek as well and then followed it up with a kiss. The first grandma settled for a pat on the head and a kiss.

Sloane looked pained, but managed to say, "Bye, Granny Kitty. Bye, Granny Pearl."

"Love you, baby!" both women called over their shoulders as they power-walked off down the street together.

Sloane stared at Amelia as though she had snot smeared all over her face.

Which Amelia *prayed* wasn't the case.

"*I* am dressed as the great British detective Sherlock Holmes." Amelia tried to look as haughty as Sloane. It probably didn't work. Sweat rolled down her back, thanks to all of the wool tweed, and she could feel her hair bushing out with humidity. Meanwhile Sloane stood there with *her* hair swept up into a silky high ponytail, her clothing so neat and clean she might have just stepped out of Instagram.

"Yeah, I got the Sherlock Holmes thing." Still, Sloane stared at her. "I just don't get *why*."

"I'm working on our project," Amelia snapped.

"And you have to wear a costume to do that?"

Before Amelia could say something witty and cutting (which was just as well since she was having trouble thinking of anything either witty or cutting), someone roared up on a motorcycle. They screeched to a halt in the empty parking space in front of the library.

The person was dressed from chin to toe in leather with a shiny black helmet to top it all off. A German shepherd sat in the sidecar. He was also decked out in leather, along with a pair of goggles. The rider cut the engine, hopped down from the bike, and swept off the helmet.

To reveal Belinda Gomez, the children's and young adult librarian.

"'Sup?" she asked them casually as she unharnessed her dog, Bunny. He woofed a greeting at them too.

"Um," said Amelia.

"Er," said Sloane.

The librarian tucked her helmet under her arm so she could unlock the door for them. "Looking to check out some books?"

"Not exactly," Amelia and Sloane both said at the exact same moment in the exact same grim tone.

Sloane made a face and confessed, "We're . . . here to get an early start on Mr. Roth's project. I guess. I mean, I am, at least. And Amelia says she is."

No.

No.

No, no, no, no, NO!

Deep down, Amelia had known it from the moment she'd laid eyes on the other girl and her grandmas. But she'd been hoping that maybe Sloane was here to just check out books on how fabulous it was to be supercool and popular.

Belinda led them into the darkened library and flipped on the lights. Shimmying out of her leather riding gear, she revealed that she wore a T-shirt that read: READ OR DIE.

Amelia was pretty sure she meant it. Her mom said book circulation was *way* up since Belinda took over.

They followed the librarian and her dog up the stairs to a bright and sunny room. Not that either the brightness or sunniness did anything to improve Amelia's mood.

"All of the old newspapers are on microfilm." Belinda held up a round cartridge that looked a bit like a small film reel. "Here's how you thread it into the machine. You use these gears to flip through the different issues, this dial to adjust the zoom, and . . . Hey, you guys *did* say you're working together, right?"

Amelia realized that she and Sloane were standing as far apart from each other as they could possibly get. They might also—possibly—have been scowling at each other. Under Belinda's stern glare, they immediately stopped and scooted closer together.

"We were standing apart so we could see what you were doing," Amelia lied.

"Hmmm . . ." Belinda narrowed her eyes at them. "You

looked like two people getting ready to yell at each other. You know there's no yelling or fighting allowed in the library, right?"

"But you're a biker. Don't bikers break the rules?"

"Not in my library, they don't," Belinda said pointedly, then left with Bunny to get coffee. Or whatever it was that biker librarians did.

Like stringing up by their thumbs people who returned overdue books and taking a tire iron to the kneecaps of anyone who caused a ruckus by fighting with her partner over a microfilm machine.

"Let's see what we can find out." Sloane sat directly in front of that microfilm machine, her hands on the controls.

Pushed off to the side, Amelia had to drag up a second chair. Consulting the packet of notes Mr. Roth had given them, she said, "We're looking for August twentieth, 1887."

Sloane whizzed through old issues of the *Fulton County Expositor* at a rate that made Amelia dizzy. Just when Amelia thought she'd have to stop looking or else throw up, Sloane screeched to a halt. "Found it."

Leaning forward, both girls peered at the headlines:

Shocking Discovery at the Hoäl House!
Safe Blown Apart!
Millions of Dollars Missing

Addison Oldfield and his carpentry crew arrived at the Hoäl mansion this morning to make a shocking discovery. Inside the millionaire's first-floor study,

Jacob Hoäl's safe had been blown apart. The wreckage was strewn about the room for all to see.

At first, no one knew what to make of this alarming turn of events. Soon, however, suspicion fell on no other than Thomas Zimmerman, one of Mr. Oldfield's finest craftsmen and Mr. Hoäl's partner in his first, ill-fated business: Hoäl and Zimmerman's Traveling Circus. The fine Mr. Hoäl had soon seen that lowly circus for the shady business that it was and went on to make a fortune for himself by investing in stocks and bonds.

When the circus went bankrupt under Zimmerman's careless guidance, his generous friend was kind enough to secure him a place in Mr. Oldfield's employ. The talented but dishonest Zimmerman had not shown up for work that day. Though Zimmerman was of worthless character and well known around town to be lazy, it was unusual that he would not want to at least collect his week's pay.

"Hang on," Sloane said. "This Thomas guy wasn't just a clown? He was a carpenter and built stuff, too?"

"When did Mr. Roth say he was a clown?" Amelia didn't remember anything about that.

Sloane shrugged sheepishly. "I just assumed. I mean, he ended up being a bad guy. So, I figured if he was going to be anything in a circus, it would be a clown."

"I like clowns," Amelia said. Sloane gave her that you've-got-snot-on-your-face look again but didn't say anything.

They both went back to reading.

Injured Zimmerman
Seeks the Assistance
of Dr. Barber

Jacob and Lucretia Hoäl left for a week in Chicago last night on the 8:00 p.m. train. Neighbors reported hearing a loud noise from the mansion around 9:15 p.m. but assumed it was Oldfield and his men finishing their work.

At 9:45 p.m., an injured Zimmerman arrived at the house of local physician Dr. Theodore Barber. He had injuries to his face and hands from an explosion. Upon seeing him, the good doctor cried out in horror, demanding to know what had happened. Ever a liar, Zimmerman claimed to have been blowing up a large boulder on the Hoäl estate.

The doctor tended generously to his patient, expecting no payment as Zimmerman was well known around town to be dishonest and lazy.

Now Amelia had a problem with what they'd read.

"That's twice the paper has said that this Zimmerman guy was well known around town for being lazy." Amelia crossed her arms.

"So?" Sloane asked.

"So, sometimes people get called things that they aren't." *Like "Yeti,"* Amelia thought, though she clamped her mouth shut, refusing to say it.

Sloane shifted about uneasily in her seat but didn't say

anything. She seemed like she wanted to, but she didn't. When Sloane still hadn't adjusted the microfilm reader so they could see more, Amelia reached over and did it herself.

Where Is Zimmerman?

Due to the nature of Zimmerman's wounds, the good doctor provided him with sleeping syrup. It was far more than the monster deserved and brought about a deep and long sleep. Dr. Barber has sworn that Zimmerman was still unconscious upon the living room sofa as late as one o'clock this afternoon. However, while the doctor was seeing another patient, Zimmerman ran off. Soon after, he was spotted boarding the 1:20 p.m. train for Chicago, no doubt along with the missing jewelry. Suspicion fell on him too late to stop his escape. Deputies have been alerted throughout Ohio, Indiana, and Illinois to check the trains coming into their stations. This devil will not long escape the grasp of the law.

Meanwhile, the honorable Hoäl family is on their way back from Chicago and expected to arrive in town shortly.

"Oh," Sloane said.

"'Oh' what?" Amelia asked.

"The train collision must not have happened yet. At least, no one seemed to know about it, if it did."

Amelia double-checked the date at the top of the newspaper. August 20, 1887. That was the day Mr. Roth had said the trains collided, killing Jacob, Lucretia, and Thomas. And leaving the fate of the missing jewels a mystery.

"'Five o'clock edition,'" Amelia read at the top of the paper. Then she scrolled forward to the next newspaper and read it. "'August 20, 1887. *Nine* o'clock edition.' How many newspapers did they put out each day?"

"Three or four." Belinda had come into the room to check on them, a cup of coffee in one hand and Bunny trotting next to her.

"That's a lot of newspaper," Amelia observed.

"Well, newspapers were sort of like the social media of the day. Something would happen, and the newspapers would print a new edition and hand it out. Lot harder for messages to go viral. But some of the articles could be every bit as mean as some people are in their postings today. They'd stick to the facts, but that didn't mean they were always nice about it."

"Yeah, I noticed that," Amelia said grimly.

The librarian left, though Bunny stayed behind to flop his head onto Amelia's lap and whine for some attention. Or maybe he smelled the peanut-butter-and-pickle sandwiches in her pocket.

Either way, Amelia reached down and scratched him behind the ears as both girls turned their attention back to the microfilm reader. Sloane printed off copies of what they'd already read, and then they started in on the nine o'clock edition's headline. It screamed:

Horrific Train Accident Claims Life of Prominent Wauseon Businessman!

"I guess everyone knows now," Amelia said, as though it had all just happened. In a strange way, it almost felt like it *had* just happened. She found herself caring about the unlucky Hoäl family. Who had woken up one morning thinking they were living the best life ever in their big mansion, only for two of them to be dead and the third one to be an orphan by sunset that same day. She also felt bad for the way everyone kept insulting Thomas Zimmerman. It was clear that the newspaper reporters didn't like him and that struck a chord in Amelia's very sore heart.

Farther down the page, there was another headline:

By Bizarre Coincidence, Wanted Thief Dies in Same Crash as His Victims

"Forget coincidence, that's just plain unlucky," Sloane said.

"That's beyond unlucky," Amelia agreed, feeling sad but her eyes shining with the drama of it all. Bunny looked up at her curiously and licked his nose. "That's like unlucky times a *thousand*. No doubt Zimmerman was feeling remorse over his *dreadful* crime. He caught that train so he could throw himself at Jacob's feet in Chicago and beg for his forgiveness, *weeping* and tearing at his hair. He was traveling toward his redemption, only to have it snatched from him—just as the Hoäl's lives were snatched from them."

Amelia trailed off, her voice catching in her throat. She thought what she'd said was terribly moving. In fact, it would make the perfect voice-over, if she decided to go with sound.

However, Sloane stared at her in unflattering disbelief.

"Why do you talk like that?" Sloane demanded in exasperation. "You sound so weird!"

"I don't sound weird, I sound dramatic!" Amelia could feel the heat rising to her face as Bunny slid off her lap. She wrenched her phone out of the selfie stick and jammed it back into her pocket. She didn't think she wanted this filmed.

"No, just weird!" Sloane snapped loudly as Bunny grumbled next to them. "You know, we were getting along just fine. You were acting normal and I was thinking that maybe we could actually work together. And then you have to go and talk like that!"

"What? Just because I can see an interesting story in things?" Amelia jumped to her feet. "Just because I have an imagination?"

"No, because you talk like a weirdo!" Sloane got to her feet too, eyes flashing. "This is why other kids keep calling you 'Yeti'! If you'd just stop acting strange for a while, they'd forget all about you and stop doing it!"

Sloane's words sliced right through to Amelia's heart. As Bunny let out a single, scolding bark, the world waivered through tears in Amelia's eyes.

"People call me names because I'm *myself*!" Amelia shouted. The tears spilled over and ran down her cheeks. "What they really want is for me not to exist at all!"

"Don't be so dramatic!"

"I'm not! You want me to stop being me!"

"Would it really be such a bad thing not to be yourself?"

Now Sloane was shouting too. "Don't you get that it's better for *everyone* not to be themselves? That way, no one can make fun of the real you, you dramatic weirdo idiot!"

Bunny threw back his head and howled.

"You're the weirdo!"

"*You're* the weirdo!"

"That's it." Belinda walked in, yanked the microfilm out of the machine, and tucked the box of cartridges under her arm. Bunny scuttled behind her legs for protection. "You two are done."

"What?" Sloane gasped in outrage. Amelia was so mortified that she couldn't form any words. "You can't do that to us!"

"I can, and I will." Belinda pointed toward the door. "Out!"

"What did we do?" Sloane protested as the librarian and her dog ushered them down the stairs. Several library patrons clutched books to their chests and gaped at Sloane and Amelia as they passed by. Amelia had the horrible feeling that the two of them had been yelling so loudly that everyone in the building had heard them.

"Created a scene. Disturbed the other library patrons. Behaved recklessly around a very expensive piece of equipment." Belinda ticked off their crimes on her fingers. "And frightened my dog."

Bunny whined as though to confirm this point.

"We'll be good," Amelia sobbed. "Please don't throw us out!"

But Belinda swung open the front glass doors and crossed her arms.

Amelia didn't want to tangle with a librarian who was also in a biker gang. She slinked out onto the sidewalk.

After a moment, Sloane stomped after her.

"I'll be in your classroom on Monday with all of the information you need," Belinda told them coldly. "Maybe then you'll manage to not scream at each other."

Yanking the door shut after her, she went back inside.

"This is all your fault!" Sloane told Amelia. "You and your annoying costumes!"

"*My* fault?" Amelia slurred through her tears. "All *you* had to do was not be a jerk!"

"*I* wasn't the jerk!" Sloane said furiously. "There's no way I can work with you! I'm emailing Mr. Roth and telling him that."

"You go right ahead, because I'm doing the same thing *right now*." Amelia pulled out her phone.

"Good!"

"Good!"

Both girls marched away from each other, Sloane toward downtown and Amelia toward the baseball diamonds at the far end of Elm Street.

Had that really been the end of things, it would have been zemblanitatious for the person who had set this whole project in motion. No one else working on the assignment would have discovered the clues that had been left behind over a hundred years before.

To get things back on track, it would take more than serendipity.

It would take two people apologizing to each other.

Two *seventh* graders.

Who both thought they were right.

4

A Museum Heist

Sloane didn't email Mr. Roth. Instead, as soon as she stomped around the corner of Fulton Street, she smacked right into both of her grannies. They were power-walking another lap around the downtown. As if the sidewalks in front of all the nineteenth-century storefronts was some sort of racetrack. Usually Nanna Tia—Sloane's great-granny—walked with them, but after Sloane's mom died, she'd started up an illegal bingo business in her living room. Now it was so successful that it took up most of her time.

"Sloane-y!" Granny Pearl and Granny Kitty both cried in delight. Cheek-pinching followed, as though they hadn't seen her in months.

"Erf." Sloane managed to pull her face free with as much dignity as she could muster. When Grampy Osburn passed away four years ago, Granny Pearl had moved from Columbus to Wauseon to live with Sloane's mom's mom and grandma. At the time, her dad had predicted it would be trouble.

"You don't think they'll get along?" Sloane's mom had asked.

Dad had shaken his head. "No, I think they'll get along *too* well."

Four years and that illegal bingo operation later, Sloane understood what he meant. She and her dad worried there might be an FBI raid at any moment.

Of course, right now, Sloane had bigger problems than the FBI. Because Mac Attack Snyder stood across the street by Sullivan's Restaurant. Smirking, she lowered her phone.

"Oh no." Sloane briefly closed her eyes. "She's taken a picture of you pinching my cheeks."

Of all the luck! She could just imagine the snaps. *Baby Sloane-y getting her cheeks pinched! Goo-goo, ga-ga, Baby Sloane!*

Well, that was one way to get everyone to forget about Amelia the Yeti. Which Sloane supposed she deserved. She'd promised the memory of her mom that she'd be nice to the girl the next time Sloane met her. A promise Sloane had promptly broken as soon as she saw Amelia in that cringey Sherlock Holmes getup. Even though she could hear her mom say in her head, *Cool costume! That's totally something right out of* Doctor Who*!*

This was clearly divine punishment for it. And for starting the whole yeti business in the first place. (Accidentally or not.)

Opening her eyes, Sloane found Mackenzie bearing down on her, still grinning.

Granny Kitty and Granny Pearl swung their heads from one girl to the other, eyes going beady.

"Why, is that little Tootie Snyder?" Granny Pearl cried sweetly, clasping her hands together in delight.

Mackenzie froze just as she reached the curb, and went white as a sheet.

"It *is,* Pearl!" Granny Kitty cried. "We play bingo with your grandma Snyder, you know! She just loves to tell us all about her granddaughter, Tootie."

"Got her nickname from the great big farts she used to do when she was a toddler," Granny Pearl continued, as though farts were the most delightful thing in the world to talk about. "Apparently she'd cry, 'Uh-oh! I tooted!' and then laugh herself silly. So, her family started calling her 'Tootie.'"

"I, um, don't go by Tootie anymore." Mackenzie could not possibly look any more mortified.

Seizing the moment, Granny Kitty grabbed Mac's phone and went, "Oh, Pearl! Look at that adorable picture she took of us with our Sloane-y! She's added the cutest little baby bonnet and diaper to our granddaughter!"

Before Mackenzie could grab her phone back, Granny Pearl reached forward and tapped the garbage can icon. "Let me see! Oopsie! Deleted it instead. Oh dear."

"Technology these days." Granny Kitty handed the phone back to Mackenzie. "You know how us old folks are with it."

"No problem!" Mackenzie gulped and scampered off toward the library before anyone could call her Tootie again.

"Don't worry, Sloane-y." Granny Pearl winked. "We've got your back."

With that, they power-walked off again in their matching tracksuits. Probably to lure other old people to Nanna Tia's bingo shack.

In spite of everything, Sloane rubbed at her cheek and felt ridiculously happy. It was nice to know someone's got your back.

Which was more than Amelia had at school.

Ugh. There went that ridiculously happy feeling.

Sloane slouched off home. She lived with her dad in a rambling Victorian house that looked out over Wauseon's South Park at the end of Fulton Street. The sharp edges of the old brick storefronts stopped at the county courthouse, giving way to a neighborhood of rounded cupolas and wide front porches. The park had a gazebo and big trees that had been little back around the time Thomas had been blowing up Jacob's safe and stealing his jewels.

Her parents had bought the falling-apart house when Sloane was a baby. Even though they were both orthodontists, her parents also liked to work with their hands. Except, first they were so busy with their business and taking care of Sloane that they hadn't gotten much done on it. Then her mom had gotten cancer, and they'd gotten even less work done on the house she'd loved so much.

These days it was just her dad working on it.

That's what David Osburn was doing when Sloane stomped in the front door and almost tripped over him as he sanded the foyer floor. At least, he must have been sanding it a moment before. Right now, he was holding up the still-whirring sander but seemed to have forgotten that it was there. Instead, he stared off into space.

He did that a lot these last two years. Looking back into the past. Like he was still trying to find Sloane's mom.

Realizing that Sloane was home, her dad jumped and turned the sander off.

"You're back early." He got up off of his knees and yanked off his face mask. "Everything okay?"

He asked it hesitantly, anxiety digging down into his brows. She knew he worried that one parent wouldn't be enough for her. That *he* wouldn't be enough for her.

"No! Everything's great, Dad!" Sloane gave him her widest

smile. The one she sometimes felt like she borrowed off someone with a concussion. Even though it always reassured him. "I'm just... back for some lunch!"

Her dad's face relaxed into his own relieved smile. "Great! How about if I warm up some of the lasagna Granny Pearl left us?"

"That sounds great!" Sloane beamed and followed him into the kitchen to help him dish out the lasagna and microwave it. The microwave sat on top of the plywood they had instead of counters. It had been two years, but her dad still couldn't bring himself to put in the butcher block counters her mom had picked out before she died.

Their whole house was like that—an old home filled with half-finished dreams.

"How's your project going?" her dad asked as they ate.

"Great!" Sloane lied. "I think I found some really useful information!"

"That's great!" her dad said back, smiling too.

Then they both realized that they had said the word "great" about half a dozen times in less than five minutes. That was ... less great.

"Um, Sloane?"

"Yes, Dad?"

"Would you mind if we didn't do our usual pizza-and–*Doctor Who* thing next Saturday?" her dad asked nervously. Seeing the astonished look on Sloane's face, he quickly added, "It's just that I have this work . . . thing. The Northwest Ohio Orthodontist Association is having a banquet at the Barn Restaurant over in Archbold and..."

"No, no—that's fine!" Sloane reassured him before he felt like he needed to tell her all about his super boring orthodontist dinner. "In fact, it's great!"

Ugh. That word again.

"Great." He nodded.

"Yeah, great."

It was not, in fact, great. Suddenly. Sloane already felt like she was sitting on the couch all by herself. Empty air where her mom should be on one side, and now empty air on the other side where her dad normally sat. Who was she going to watch *Doctor Who* with? Who was going to reassure her that bacon and banana peppers were neither weird nor gross pizza toppings?

But her dad tried so hard. And he was so sad so much of the time.

How could she ever tell him anything wasn't great?

After lunch, Sloane grabbed her bicycle and rode across town to the Fulton County Historical Society. Someone from the museum was also supposed to be at their class on Monday, but Sloane figured she could find out some stuff now. Then she'd text it to Amelia to try to make peace between them.

However, arriving at the historical society, she felt like she'd ridden backward in time about six months to last Halloween. The historical society was housed in a very old building that had once been a creepy school, then a creepy hospital, and finally a creepy apartment building before being turned into a creepy museum. There were supposed to be ghosts all over it. Probably a few evil clowns as well, because it was that sort of building.

The sort of building Sloane was about to go into.

Alone.

Well, except for the ghosts and possible clowns.

Next door to the museum, a kid of about six or seven was bouncing a basketball slowly against the driveway. It made an ominous *dun-dun-dun* sound. The boy watched open-mouthed as Sloane pulled her bike into the museum's driveway and tucked it behind a lilac bush. A WELCOME! sign hung above the wooden steps, its chain creaking eerily in the breeze. Which also stirred a few dead leaves across the planks in a not-at-all menacing way.

"It's haunted, you know," the little boy with the basketball piped up helpfully.

"Thanks." Sloane grimaced and squeezed the straps of her backpack more tightly.

"I seen 'em through the window. A creepy woman with a tall black hat and a long black dress like a witch."

"Any clowns?"

The boy shook his head. "Just witches."

Well, that was something, at least. Sloane wasn't particularly afraid of witches.

The slats groaned beneath her sneakers as she climbed the steps. Taking a deep breath, she marched across the front porch and thrust open the door. Inside the foyer, thick walls blocked most of the noise from outside.

However, someone *inside* the museum was chanting in Latin. At least, Sloane thought it was Latin. Some sort of creepy-sounding language, anyhow.

Sloane gulped.

"He-he-hello?" she called.

The chanting continued. It was coming from two rooms away on her right, Sloane thought. It was probably a ghost teacher giving lessons in a dead language.

"Hello?" Sloane squeaked.

People called "Slayer" did not run from ghosts. Knees knocking, Sloane forced herself forward. Into a room filled from floor to ceiling with books behind beveled glass doors. The research room, she thought. Which was good because she was here to do research.

What was less good was that a wide doorway led into *another* room. This one filled with rather horrifying taxidermy animals.

And a witch in a long black dress and pointed hat.

A ghost witch. Just like the little boy next door had said.

Slayer Sloane scuttled backward, her feet sliding on the Turkish carpet. Instead of escaping, she fell against the massive oak desk in the middle of the room.

The witch turned around, spotting her . . .

. . . and revealing herself to actually be a *him*self.

"I'm, uh, Milton Unserios. The museum's curator?" The witch said it so nervously that it turned into a question. Like he wasn't entirely sure if he was the curator or not and was hoping that Sloane could confirm it for him. "The museum, uh, doesn't usually get many visitors on Saturdays. And sometimes I, um, get bored."

Her terror draining away, Sloane realized that Milton wore a very expensive-looking Harry Potter robe and hat. In his hand was an equally pricey wand, while a pair of round spectacles perched upon his nose. His maroon-and-gold bow tie proclaimed Milton to be Gryffindor. Which Sloane personally doubted.

The museum curator was definitely a Hufflepuff all the way.

"You won't tell anyone I was playing around with the stuffed owl, will you?" Milton asked anxiously, sweeping the peaked hat off his head. He gestured at an enormous taxidermic barn owl he had taken out from beneath its protective glass dome.

"I definitely promise," Sloane assured him as she got back up onto her feet. No way she was telling anyone about this. Ever. "I'm Sloane Osburn, and I'm here from Mr. Roth's class about the missing Hoäl jewels."

Milton tugged at his bow tie and looked confused. "I didn't think anyone was actually going to come *here*. No one ever comes here on the weekend. I thought I was supposed to go out to the middle school on Monday. I'm quite looking forward to it, you know. I don't get to go on many field trips!"

"My partner and I are just trying to get a leg up on the competition," Sloane said as she slid her backpack off her shoulders. "I'm here to collect some information so she and I can get right to work on Monday."

The museum curator sorted through all the other Harry Potter stuff strewn about the place; from a Slytherin mug to Hufflepuff and Ravenclaw pens to a Marauder's Map background on his desktop. Finally, he came up with a dreadfully boring-looking book called *Notorious and Illustrious Citizens of Fulton County, Along with a List of Their Crimes and Accomplishments*. Milton flipped it open to a yellowed page. At the top, there was a picture of a group of people in circus costumes. They stood before an elaborately carved wooden wagon painted with the words HOÄL and ZIMMERMAN'S CIRCUS. Sloane read the caption, and just as she had suspected, Thomas was dressed like a clown. Jacob wore a plain suit and looked like he wanted to be somewhere, anywhere, else.

"Thomas built the wagon," Milton enthused. "He was actually quite a talented carpenter. If he'd stuck to that, he probably would have done very well for himself. Maybe he wouldn't have ended up as rich as Jacob, but he'd have made money."

"What about the circus?" Sloane asked. "Why'd he leave that?"

"Because he didn't have any choice." Milton tugged on his bow tie again. "Thomas wasn't a businessman. Without Jacob's guidance, the circus soon went bankrupt, while Jacob became wealthy. In the end, Thomas had to come back to town and beg Jacob for work on his house."

That was kind of sad. Sloane opened her mouth to say so, when a roar caught her attention from the street outside. Going over to the window, Sloane and Milton both saw a motorcycle screech to a halt along the curb outside the building. Its rider wore black leather, while a large German shepherd panted happily in the sidecar.

No.

No.

Maybe all of the librarians at the Wauseon Public Library rode motorcycles and had large dogs as their best friends, Sloane thought hopefully. Maybe they were a librarian gang.

Then the rider hopped onto the sidewalk and took off her helmet.

Yup. It was Belinda Gomez.

If Sloane had known the word "zemblanity," she doubtless would have used it. For, in her mind, this wasn't just bad luck. This was beyond bad luck. This was—this was . . . this was someone *not minding her own business*, that's what this was.

However, Sloane didn't know the word "zemblanity." So, rather than gasping it out loud, she started looking for an escape route.

"Hey, you don't have a back door, do you?" Sloane asked, but it was already too late. Belinda bounded up the stairs and burst through the foyer door with Bunny hot on her heels.

"Yo, Milton!" she shouted. "I'm here for the . . ."

The librarian stopped midsentence, Bunny skidding to a halt next to her. She took in Sloane and Milton looking like he'd just wandered in from the teachers' lounge at Hogwarts.

"What's going on here?" Belinda demanded. "What have you done to Milton?"

"Er," said Milton.

"Gotta go!" said Sloane, booking it out of there before Belinda could get cross with her again. She didn't really know that Belinda would, but the librarian was a little scary and seemed like she might turn Sloane's hide into a book.

For those uncertain about where one's hide is located, it's typically located on the part of the body used for sitting. For it to get turned into a book, it would most definitely require zemblanity, not just bad luck.

Once again, Sloane didn't know the word "zemblanity." But she did know she liked her hide right where it was.

She didn't stop running until she reached the Civil War

monument on top of North Park's hill. Then she leaned against it to rest, kind of embarrassed with herself. People nicknamed "Slayer" didn't run from librarians just because they were afraid they'd get a scolding. Granted, Belinda was a biker librarian and might take bookbinding tape to Sloane's face, but still.

Regardless, it was lucky she did so, as it allowed Sloane to spot a bit of movement in the bushes along the side of the museum.

Someone was hiding in the lilac bush that sagged against the museum's front porch.

Someone in a black sweater, black leggings, black hat, and black Halloween eye mask.

Amelia disentangled herself from the pale purple blossoms and slid along the north side of the building with her arms splayed. She had tied her phone to her forehead. With a sinking feeling, Sloane realized Amelia was probably filming everything she did.

Which, for some reason, appeared to involve breaking into the museum. Probably because it was more dramatic than just going up and knocking on the door.

The little boy who had been shooting baskets in his driveway stopped to watch Amelia with his mouth hanging open.

Amelia was short enough to skim right under the side windows without being seen. From her vantage point looking into the east windows, Sloane could tell that Milton and Belinda were still talking in the front room. Amelia continued until she was beneath the open window into the back room. The one that contained the taxidermic animals with which Milton had been playing Harry Potter.

The girl reached up, her fingers just hooking the windowsill.

Amelia tugged with all of her might, feet scrabbling against the whitewashed brick siding, trying to find a toehold.

Belinda glanced over her shoulder toward the room full of stuffed animals, but kept on talking to Milton.

Sloane's heart skipped a beat.

If Amelia got caught, she might get into trouble. Maybe not— but maybe.

But Sloane had already caused Amelia to get into trouble once today already. That tugged at her conscience even before her imaginary mom started worrying about Amelia hurting herself. *Remember how I broke my wrist falling off a porch when I was kid?* Sloane's mom said in her mind. *If Amelia falls, she could break something too.*

Ugh. Now Sloane had *two* images in her mind to worry about. A sobbing Amelia getting lectured by Biker Belinda and a crying Amelia getting loaded into an ambulance.

Amelia's feet skidded against the side of the museum. She almost got a leg up over the windowsill, only to have her feet slip. Down she went with a "Whoa!" loud enough for Sloane to hear it across the street in the park.

Sloane flinched and sucked in her breath, convinced Amelia had broken something. Fortunately, the other girl hopped to her feet and brushed herself off, clearly uninjured.

Less fortunately, Belinda and Milton both went into the back room to look out the window.

Sloane's heart skipped *another* beat, but Amelia pressed herself flat against the wall beneath the windowsill.

The historian, the librarian, and the librarian's dog all looked out, but they just saw the boy holding his basketball. He was kind enough to shove his finger up his nose and announce, "There's ghost witches in there, you know."

Clearly, he was talking to Amelia, but Milton and Belinda must have thought he was talking to them. They waved at him and then went back into the front room again.

Luck had absolutely nothing at all to do with what happened next. Sloane didn't want to get into trouble, but she didn't want Amelia to get hurt or in trouble either.

And she *did* want to make things up to the other girl. For a moment, Sloane tugged at her ponytail, torn between two choices: Walk away like she'd never seen Amelia, or go along with the girl's weird plan? Stay out of trouble, or risk getting into it? Keep on ignoring Amelia and hope things would get better, or actually help her?

Harder and harder, Sloane pulled on her hair as the seconds ticked away. She knew what her mom would tell her to do. She knew what Mackenzie would tell her to do.

And then she knew what Sloane would do.

She sped down the hill to help Amelia.

She caught the other girl as she tried to climb up onto the window sill again. Sloane looped her fingers together, grabbed Amelia's foot, and gave her a lift upward.

"There's a book in there called *Notorious and Illustrious Citizens of Fulton County*. There are a bunch of pages about the case," Sloane babbled. "I'll buy you enough time to take pictures of them. Oh, and there's a photo of Jacob and Thomas together with their circus. Maybe get a picture of that, too."

Before Amelia could say anything back, Sloane pushed her up and over the windowsill. As she had expected, the other girl lost her balance and crashed to the floor. Sloane winced, praying that Amelia hadn't broken anything. Mainly herself.

From somewhere inside the museum, Belinda's suspicious voice said, "Hey, what was that?"

Turning around, Sloane snatched the basketball from the kid who still had his finger jammed up his nose. Trying not to think about the fact that he'd just been touching the ball, she dashed around the side of the building and up onto the porch.

Where she began to dribble loudly against the porch boards.

"Sloane Osburn, *what* are you doing?" Belinda asked in exasperation as she and Milton ran outside. The librarian had his wand raised like he planned to cast some sort of spell.

Bunny barked and wagged his tail, clearly wanting to play.

"I, um, do sports when I need to think." Sloane pounded the ball loudly against the porch floor. Out of the corner of her eye, she could see Amelia through the window. The other girl had gotten unsteadily to her feet but didn't seem to be hurt. Now she struggled to remove her phone from where she had tied it to her head so she could take pictures of the book.

"What do you need to think about?" Milton asked in bewilderment.

"Oh. Um. All sorts of things." Like the fact that Sloane was helping her partner commit what might quite possibly be an actual crime. Breaking into a museum couldn't be legal, even if you didn't steal anything. The FBI might bust her, along with Nanna Tia and her bingo operation.

"What's going on here?" An all-too-familiar voice called from down the street.

Sloane caught the basketball in her arms. If her heart had been skipping beats before, now it decided to give up and play dead. That voice belonged to Mr. Roth.

Because he was walking up the street toward them.

With Principal Stuckey next to him.

Sloane closed her eyes. Maybe if she kept them closed long enough, the adults around her would grow bored and wander off to find some other children to torment.

"Sloane, why are you playing basketball on the museum's front porch?" Mr. Roth asked, still down on the sidewalk. Bunny had run out to greet him and Principal Stuckey, keeping them down on the sidewalk.

Sloane opened up her eyes.

"It helps me think." Which was not a lie. Right now, it was definitely helping her to think that this was all a very bad idea.

At least none of the adults were positioned so they could see Amelia as she ransacked the museum for the book. Milton and Belinda still had their backs to the window, and Mr. Roth and Principal Stuckey were too far down the sidewalk.

Of course, if they walked closer, they'd *definitely* see Amelia.

So, like Bunny, Sloane ran down to greet these two new bothersome adults. The other two already-bothersome adults followed hot on her heels.

"Mr. Roth, I think it's really not fair that you're requiring me and Amelia to work together," Sloane said. "We just don't get along. Forcing us to work together means that neither one of us is going to do as good of a job as we would have if you'd just let us work alone. We can't work together."

Except, of course, they were working together right now.

She probably shouldn't mention that fact.

"Yes, Principal Stuckey already told me about the scene you and Amelia caused at the library," Mr. Roth said pointedly.

"What?" Sloane gasped. Why did her principal know about that?

"I was checking out a new book on Mennonite cooking!" Principal Stuckey held it up. "I was looking for a good snickerdoodle recipe. You know, Pence, Sloane here might have a point. We want the students to learn as much as possible from this, not fight with each other."

"And part of what they will learn is how to work together," Mr. Roth said firmly, giving Bunny a final pat on the head and walking past Sloane, toward the museum. "Now, let's finish up the last details on this project before anyone else shows up early to work on it! I must say, I love the enthusiasm you seem to have for this project, Sloane."

Sloane winced as they headed over to the porch stairs. She opened her mouth to say something—anything—before they spotted Amelia in the window. But she couldn't think of a single thing.

Fortunately, she didn't need to.

Amelia saw the group of adults before they saw her and dove out the open window. As they went inside, she landed with a crash in the bush.

Tossing the basketball back to the nose-picker, Sloane ran over and tugged Amelia free. The black cap had fallen off her head. Leaves and twigs poked out of her curls, and she'd torn the elbow on her sweater.

"Are you all right?" Sloane gasped, worried that she wasn't.

But Amelia triumphantly held up her phone to show a picture of *Notorious and Illustrious Citizens of Fulton County.*

"Got it," she said smugly.

Working together, they'd actually pulled this off. Neither Mackenzie nor Mylie nor Kylee would have been able to do it. Mackenzie wouldn't have had the interest, Kylee the imagination, and Mylie the ability to stay quiet long enough.

An awkward silence hung in the air between them, offering Sloane two choices: ask for the pictures and go her own way . . .

Or work with Amelia.

This wasn't about serendipity or zemblanity.

This was all on Sloane—and Amelia—to decide.

"Look, I'm sorry about what I said earlier," Sloane said. "Do . . . you want to work together on this?"

For a moment, Amelia stood perfectly still.

Then, she nodded her head.

With that, they both moved one step closer to the jewels.

And one step closer to having those jewels taken away from them.

5

Working Together Actually Works

Depending on how you look at it, when Sloane told Amelia that she was sorry and asked if she wanted to work together, it could be either serendipity or zemblanity. It was serendipitous for the person who'd set the whole school project in motion, though that person didn't know it yet. On the other hand, it was somewhat zemblanitatious for Sloane and Amelia. Had Sloane just said an awkward "bye" and slinked off, neither she nor Amelia would have found themselves pinned down in a cemetery by an attacker with a slingshot and acorns.

Of course, they also wouldn't have figured out what happened to the missing Hoäl jewels, either.

Amelia wasn't thinking about either good luck or bad luck as she followed Sloane back to her house on the other side of town. After Sloane told her about being sorry, she honestly had no idea what to say.

No one had ever apologized to her before.

Not one single time.

Certainly not the kids at school. Not even her family. Definitely not her family. It probably had never occurred to her parents or siblings that they even *could* be wrong.

About anything. Ever.

Was this what having a friend felt like? Amelia wondered hesitantly. She knew that saying "I'm sorry" wasn't exactly the same thing as saying "Hey! Let's be friends!"

But it was still the closest anyone had ever come to it for Amelia. As Sloane walked next to her, walking her bike so they could go the same speed, Amelia's imagination conjured up all sorts of dreams. Sloane watching one of her YouTube videos and telling her how great it was! Sloane telling off Mackenzie for laughing at Amelia! Sloane telling off the next kid who called Amelia a yeti!

Sloane admitting to Amelia that she, too, was lonely and wished she had someone who understood her.

In the ten minutes it took the two girls to walk from North Park to South Park, Amelia even had Sloane heroically standing up to Amelia's family, telling them no more sports nights ever again. Amelia pictured it with the sun setting gloriously in the distance, just like the climactic scene of a movie.

Her legs felt positively wobbly with joy as she climbed the steps of Sloane's gorgeous old house in a leafy, quiet part of town. Though big, it wasn't coldly humungous like Amelia's parents' house out on the golf course. It didn't shout about how expensive it was. Instead, it was pink and green on the outside with windows that were old-fashioned beveled glass. You could tell it would be full of all sorts of useless nooks and crannies and tucked-away cupboards and reading spots. The sort of place that belonged to you, rather than just letting you live in it.

As they stepped into the foyer, Sloane said, "What do you know? He actually finished it."

She must have meant the floor, which looked newly sanded

and swept clean, ready to be polished. Amelia followed Sloane into the kitchen. Through the old windows, the grass and trees blurred together greenly. Amelia felt a bit like she was in a boat at sea.

A happy, happy boat, full of people liked by other people.

"Can you load the pictures onto my Chromebook so we can see them better?" Sloane asked, rummaging about in a great-grandmother of a refrigerator to come up with some cookie dough. "Do you like chocolate chip?"

"Is the answer to that ever no?" Amelia found the Chromebook's USB cable and attached her phone to it.

"Ha—my dad doesn't like chocolate, if you can believe it. Mom said she almost didn't marry him for that reason." Sloane laughed, only to have the smile quickly slide from her face.

Immediately, the warm haze that had curled around Amelia as she imagined Sloane becoming her friend vanished. Instead, a coldness crept up from the holes in her soul filled with shame. She remembered that last time they had discussed Sloane's mom back in April at the library. When she had babbled all of those mortifying things because Mackenzie and Sloane's other friends had made her so nervous.

She'd probably ruined whatever chance she had of being Sloane's friend back then. Still, the words "I'm sorry" swelled up into Amelia's mouth as Sloane twisted her ponytail anxiously. However, before Amelia could actually say them, Sloane changed the subject. "Hey, want to see something cool?"

Sloane went over to a super old-fashioned oven. She pulled out a box of matches and opened the door. Then she struck a match and reached inside, holding it close to a spout. A blue flame whisked out of the spout, heating up the oven. Sloane snatched her hand back, shook the match out, and closed the oven door.

"That's how we have to light our oven because it's so old." Sloane tried to look modest.

"Wow!" Not only was Amelia impressed, she was grateful to have the subject changed. "You just turn ours on by hitting a button. It's pretty boring."

Sloane slid the cookies into the oven. "Let's take a look at those pictures and see if we can come up with anything good. After all of the people we've annoyed today, we'd better have something good for Monday."

"How do you feel about making a video instead of a slideshow, the way most kids are gonna do it?" Amelia asked hesitantly. Sloane seemed to really want to work together, but the Miller-Poe family didn't do teamwork. In fact, *Never Give Up! Never Give In! Never Let Anyone Else Have Opinions!* could very well be their family motto.

Sloane took a deep breath and yanked on her ponytail a few times. It seemed to take a bit of effort, but she said, "Sure, let's do a video."

"All right, then." Amelia relaxed. She pulled up the first photo she'd taken of the *Notorious and Illustrious Citizens of Fulton County* book. "Let's take a look at what this has to say about Thomas Zimmerman."

Notorious and Illustrious Citizens of Fulton County used fonts that were a lot less interesting than the old *Fulton County Expositor*. Still, it had quite a bit to say.

Thomas Zimmerman—
Clown, Carpenter, Criminal

Born into the wealthy Zimmerman farm family, Thomas grew up in their large farmhouse out on Old Ridge Road. As very old-fashioned people, his father and mother disapproved of dancing, card-playing, games, singing, laughing, toys, taking naps, reading books, keeping animals as pets, going to the circus, going to the theatre, and eating sweets. For obvious reasons, they were disappointed when he ran away with the circus.

"With that list, they would have been disappointed if he'd become a doctor or a lawyer!" Amelia exclaimed, feeling a sudden kinship for Thomas Zimmerman, to whom she could relate all too well since she and her family didn't see eye to eye on pretty much anything.

"Yeah, they don't exactly sound like fun people, do they?" Sloane agreed before they returned to reading.

While Zimmerman dreamed of being a clown, his first job with the circus was as a carpenter. He helped build props for the magician and knife-thrower, as well as build new wagons when the old ones broke down. It wasn't until his friend Jacob managed to save up enough money to buy the run-down circus that Thomas finally fulfilled his lifelong dream of performing as a clown. Unfortunately, when Jacob sold the circus to Thomas, Thomas proved to be an even worse manager than he was a clown. Within a few years, the circus went bankrupt and Thomas returned to Wauseon, looking for work as a carpenter.

There was a picture of a super fancy fireplace and wood-paneled walls that Thomas had carved. Rather than boring, straight lines like modern fireplaces, it looked like a sculpture. Like something that belonged in a museum. The panels looked like trees, and their branches reached out to form the leafy mantelpiece.

"I feel sort of bad for Thomas," Sloane confessed as Amelia zoomed in closer on the picture. "I know that stealing isn't great, and I know that he's the one who set in motion all of the events that ended up getting Jacob and Lucretia and a bunch of other people killed. But . . . he had a dream, you know? And somehow that all went wrong,"

"Maybe this Jacob Hoäl guy was a real jerk," Amelia said optimistically. "Perhaps he was really a dastardly villain who had done Zimmerman a terrible wrong by abandoning him in his hour of need. Perhaps, like Zimmerman's parents, he had no scope to his imagination, choosing money over friendship. The cold business world over the excitement and beauty of art and entertainment."

Getting caught up in the emotion of what she was saying, Amelia clasped her hands together, trembling. . . .

Only to realize that Sloane was wincing.

"What?" Amelia dropped her hands.

"Um, well." Sloane scrunched up her face. She seemed to be struggling to put whatever she had to say nicely. "It's just—nobody talks like that."

"Oh." Embarrassed, Amelia looked down. "I've been trying to talk sort of like the title cards they used in old silent movies. You know, the ones that would explain what was going on, since there was no sound. My grandma Suzy and I used to watch them all the time before she moved down to Florida. Talking like that makes me feel the way I felt when I watched them with her. You know...happy."

Why had she said all that? Why had she talked like they were friends? Amelia rubbed her finger along the rounded edge of the table. Why there was never a convenient bottomless pit around to toss herself into when she needed one?

"I get wanting to hold on to the things that make you happy," Sloane said quietly. Then the oven timer dinged, and she leapt up to get the cookies. She slid a hot and gooey cookie onto a plate in front of Amelia. "Forget what I said. How about if we put together a time line of events?"

Amelia nodded, so Sloane typed with one hand and ate her cookie with the other. They ended up with this:

August 19, 8:00 p.m.—The Hoäls board the train for Chicago.

August 19, 9:15 p.m.—Neighbors hear an explosion by the Hoäl house but assume the workmen are blasting away some large boulders from the property.

August 19, 9:45 p.m.—Zimmerman arrives at Dr. Barber's house. The doctor takes care of his wounds and gives him something to make him sleep.

August 20, 1:00 p.m.—Dr. Barber observes that Zimmerman is still asleep on his couch.
August 20, 1:20 p.m.—Zimmerman boards a train for Chicago.

August 20, 1:50 p.m.—The Hoäls board a train back to Wauseon.

August 20, 4:18 p.m.—The trains collide near South Bend, Indiana, killing everyone on board.

"Okay, so we have a time line, but that doesn't get us any closer to figuring out what happened to the stolen jewels." Sloane pushed the Chromebook away and made a face. "You know, it's not fair of Mr. Roth to ask us to come up with ideas about what happened. No one was able to figure it out back then, so why would we be able to now? It's really unfair. Maybe Mr. Roth is trying to find them, and he's making us do the hard work of sorting out the clues."

"Or Principal Stuckey," Amelia suggested, munching on her cookie. "Or they could be in on it together."

"Along with Milton and Belinda!"

"If so, we don't want to do *too* good of a job." Amelia laughed and handed Sloane another cookie too. "They might murder whoever gets it right so they can steal the stolen jewels all over again!"

Now they both laughed and then stopped. As they looked at each other uncertainly, Amelia said, "That's probably not what's going on."

"Yeah, probably not."

"Yeah." Sloane still looked a little uncertain, so Amelia decided to get them back on track. "Maybe that Thomas guy gave them to someone."

"Yeah, but the police would have thought of that at the time," Sloane argued. "I'm sure the police kept a close eye on anyone he knew and noticed if anyone was suddenly really wealthy. What I don't get is why Thomas got onto a train so quickly after he woke up. *And* without all of the stuff that he stole. Unless he did and someone found them in the wreckage and just never told anyone."

"I guess that's what we could suggest for our theory of what happened." Glumly, Amelia ate another cookie. "Of course, Mr. Roth will insist that we back that up with some sort of evidence or logic. But I don't know what else anyone *could* suggest."

"It's not like he had much time to hide them anywhere," Sloane agreed. "He didn't have them when he got to Dr. Barber's house, and he was on a train twenty minutes after he left it. There's no way he had enough time to get the jewels from wherever he hid them, give them to someone else, buy a train ticket, and get onto a train in that amount of time. He *had* to have hidden them before he went to Dr. Barber's house."

"About the only thing he could have done was bury it in some farm field," Amelia mused. "But if he did that, a farmer would have found it by now. Maybe they did and never told anyone? Or he could have buried it somewhere in town, too, but . . . thirty minutes isn't very long to dig a hole, hide the jewels, and get to a doctor. Especially if you're hurt and in pain."

"I wonder where Dr. Barber's house was. I mean, back at that time, the town pretty much ended here at South Park."

"What does it matter where his house was?" Amelia asked, not sure where Sloane was going with this.

"It's just—well, the old Hoäl mansion is right at the edge of town, right?"

"Right. So?"

"Burr Road is right around the corner from here. Just over there." Sloane pointed through the windows and out the backyard. Amelia turned to look, but there were trees and a couple of houses between here and there. "The Hoäl house is at the end of it, about a mile away, and it takes about twenty minutes to walk from the end of the road to here. The neighbors heard the explosion around nine fifteen, and then Thomas showed up at Dr. Barber's house half an hour later. It takes about twenty minutes to walk from there to about here. So, even if Dr. Barber lived somewhere around South Park, Thomas only had about ten minutes to hide those jewels. Maybe even less."

"So, they *have* to be somewhere between here and the Hoäl house," Amelia concluded with a sigh. "But why hasn't anyone found them? Oh!"

Amelia straightened up after her "Oh!" Her eyes took on a dreamy look that made Sloane narrow her own eyes suspiciously.

"You know what we need to do, Sloane?" Amelia whispered dramatically.

"Haven't a clue." But from the look on Amelia's face, Sloane suddenly worried that it was going to involve dynamite, a blown-apart safe, and a complete re-creation of the explosion for the dramatic purposes of their video.

"We need to go to the Hoäl house! We must examine the scene of the crime that started this tragic tale!"

Sloane sagged in relief and nodded her head.

Of course, had she known where Amelia's idea was going to lead, she might have suggested re-creating the explosion instead.

For, with their decision to visit the old Hoäl house, they moved one step closer to delivering the missing jewels into the hands of their slingshot-carrying attacker.

6

SOCIAL MEDIA UNICORNS

Amelia couldn't believe her luck that Slayer Sloane had actually gone along with her idea. She'd come up with it mainly because sneaking around the old mansion looking for clues would make for an excellent scene for their movie.

Sloane had gone along with it for a different reason. Partly, she'd just been relieved that Amelia hadn't wanted to do something dangerous. A bigger reason, however, was that it was exactly the sort of thing her mom would have suggested if she'd been here. Her mom had *always* been up for an adventure. Like the time she'd gotten some flapper dresses online and then insisted that she and Sloane wear them to Sauder Historic Village so they could wander around the 1920s section, eating too much ice cream and saying things like "This is the cat's pajamas!"

Sloane had never told Mackenzie or Kylee or Mylie about that. Mac would have made fun of her, while Kylee and Mylie would have simply stared at her like she was the weirdest person ever. Then they all would have inched away from Sloane like her nerdiness was contagious and they didn't want to catch it.

Her dad had taken Sloane back to Sauder Village after her mom died. They'd eaten ice cream cones too, but it hadn't been the same no matter how many times they reassured each other that it was great.

Of course, deciding to go check out the Hoäl house and finding a way to do it were two different things. The mansion had recently been turned into a luxury spa where people could relax and get various parts of their body peeled off. Two seventh graders couldn't just march inside and demand to see the scene of a long-ago crime.

However, the person who had actually set all of this in motion could and, in fact, *had* done just that. All that person had ended up with was wrinkly toes from soaking their feet too long and a sore face from having a layer of skin scrubbed off while the facialist enthused about how great it looked now that there was less skin cluttering it up.

That was zemblanity for you. You went in hoping to discover clues to an old crime so you could commit a new crime. Instead, you ended up paying hundreds of dollars to feel like a stewed tomato.

"Okay, I'm good with your plan," Sloane told Amelia. "But before we figure out a way into the Hoäl house without an appointment, I want to find out where Dr. Barber lived. That way, once we're at the Hoäl house, we'll know what direction Thomas went. It will help us imagine what he might have been thinking and what he might have done."

"Like getting into character!" Amelia enthused. So, they called Milton over at the Fulton County Historical Society to ask a question.

"I'm not supposed to talk to you until Monday," Milton told

Sloane. "Your teacher said I shouldn't give you an unfair advantage over your classmates."

"Come on, Milton. Wouldn't Harry help a fellow Gryffindor?"

"You're a Gryffindor?" the historian asked in surprise.

"Sure." Sloane was actually Ravenclaw, but she figured that telling a tiny lie for the greater good was exactly the sort of thing a Ravenclaw would do. "Can you tell me where Dr. Barber lived back in 1887? He was the guy who stitched up Thomas Zimmerman."

"Oh, that's easy. He lived at 435 East Park Street. Why?"

"No reason." Sloane hung up. To Amelia, she said, "That's two houses down from here! I was right! The jewels *have* to still be between here and the Hoäl mansion! But how are we going to get in there to start our investigation?"

"I think I might know a way," Amelia groaned, closing her eyes in pain.

There was a front desk armed by a lady with a very tight bun and very suspicious eyes who did *not* like children very much. She was so skinny and had such a huge jaw that she looked exactly like a marionette.

Amelia knew this because her mom had taken her and Ashley there for a spa day last winter break. Puppet Lady had glared at her like she thought Amelia might finger-paint the walls with jam or otherwise act like a toddler.

Honestly, it sort of made her *want* to finger-paint the walls with jam.

Still, that evening after the Miller-Poe family finished up another rousing round of golf, Amelia took one for the team. Not the Miller-Poe team. The Sloane-Amelia team.

"Say, Mom." Amelia did the best she could to be heard as they gathered around the big, sparkling island in the big, sparkling kitchen.

"I can't believe you got an ace on that back tee," Aiden complained to Ashley, ignoring Amelia.

"Gave me a birdie," Ashley said happily. "Sorry you ended up with a bogey."

They might as well have been speaking French as far as Amelia was concerned. She tried to speak up again, louder this time. "Um, Mom?"

"Better than a double bogey!" The Judge chuckled like he'd just made a very good joke.

"Mom?"

"Now, Ashley, Aiden had a very impressive duck hook on the ninth hole," Amelia's mom said. "You have to give him that."

"HEY, EVERYBODY!" Amelia leaned forward with her arms splayed and smacked her hands against the quartz countertop. "I've got something I'd like to ask!"

Nonplussed, they all stared at her.

"Ahem," Amelia cleared her throat. "Mom, Sloane and I were wondering if you'd take us to the Hoäl mansion tomorrow. For, um, facials. And pedicures."

And possibly to pretend to blow up a safe so they could imagine what a person might think after having done so. That sort of thing.

Her mom blinked. "Why on earth do the two of you want facials and pedicures?"

Amelia would rather not explain, given that doing so would probably cause her mom to say no. Fortunately, she knew her family's biggest weakness. "Er, so we can do research. And get information that no one else in the class will have. So that our presentation will be, um, the best."

That resulted in an explosion of chatter that echoed through the vast kitchen.

Her mom snapped into competition mode, eyes glinting. "You really don't think anyone else will check it out?"

The Judge nodded approvingly. "Are you doing a slideshow? If so, solid choice! Conservative but effective."

"Ooh! I want to go too!" Ashley brightened up. "That ace chipped my nail polish."

"Me too!" Aiden bobbed his head vigorously. "You wouldn't believe what lacrosse has done to my feet. My calluses actually terrified the kids at the pool the other day."

"What?" Amelia gasped in horror, not expecting this.

"Yes, the whole family should go!" Amanda Poe seemed to think this was a brilliant idea. "We can help you get all the right information! Make sure you don't miss anything that might impress Mr. Roth!"

"No!" Amelia wilted down into her chair, suddenly wishing Sloane was here. The other girl would have known what to say to change their minds. Or, at the very least, sympathized with Amelia about how overbearing her family was. "That won't be necessary!"

But apparently it was. Even the Judge was dragged along, though he protested that he didn't want to get his calluses removed. However, Amelia's mom said that his troll feet were ruining the hardwood floors.

So, to top everything else off, Amelia had that image to haunt her nightmares.

We're on, Amelia texted Sloane.

You're amazing! Sloane texted back.

Amelia stared at that message for a long time. Even after she put it away, she kept pulling her phone out again all evening long so she could look at it.

No one had ever told her she was amazing before.

In fact, no one from school had ever texted her at all.

Every time she looked at it, a happy glow welled up in Amelia's chest. Not everyone thought she was some dumb yeti.

Sunday morning, the Miller-Poes picked up Sloane at her house on the way to the Hoäl mansion. When Sloane opened the door, David Osburn waved at Amelia as he polished the newly sanded foyer floor. Sloane tugged on her ponytail, which Amelia had noticed she did whenever she was nervous.

"Something wrong?" she asked as they walked toward the Miller-Poe family SUV.

"What? No! Everything's great!" Sloane gave Amelia such a big, bug-eyed smile that Amelia took a step back. Sloane immediately tried to turn it into a normal smile but only managed a grimace. "My dad is fixing up the house."

"Is that a bad thing?"

"I haven't decided yet." Sloane cast a worried look over her shoulder.

In the car, the only word Sloane managed to get out was "hi" before the rest of the Miller-Poes talked over her for the rest of the drive down Burr Road to the spa. The Hoäl mansion sat at the end of the street, surrounded by leafy trees and, beyond them, farm fields that had yet to be plowed. It was the size of a small castle and made of red brick and stone with lots of windows. Arriving through the stone gateway, the Miller-Poes tumbled out of the car and stormed the front door like a gang of Vikings.

"So. This is your family," Sloane whispered as they stepped into the two-story foyer of the Hoäl House Day Spa and Retreat.

"Yup," Amelia confirmed miserably.

"They talk a lot."

"Yup."

"And they don't listen very much."

"Nope."

"Christmas must be fun."

"'Bout like this, actually."

They'd never once gotten Amelia anything she'd actually asked for. Only things that they thought would make her smarter, healthier, prettier, and more like them.

The puppet lady was at the front desk, looking every bit as scary as Amelia remembered. She took in the loudly talking Miller-Poes and hissed, "Quiet, please! This is a place of quiet reflection and relaxation! Not a—a—a *hockey* brawl."

That brought Amelia's parents and siblings up short. Amelia's mom immediately glued on her extra-friendly businesswoman smile and proceeded to check them all in. As she did so, Sloane jerked her head toward some photographs on the wall in a way that said she wanted Amelia to look at them too. Without her family noticing.

As casually as she could, Amelia joined her. In the middle of the wall, there was a large picture of what the mansion looked like now: gorgeous and expensive. All around it, there were old photographs of what it looked like over the years. For most of them, that meant a falling-apart mess. Large letters above the new picture read *If we can do this to a house, imagine what we could do to you!*

Amelia did imagine it. She imagined scary spa workers taking power sanders and drills to her face and decided she'd rather not.

"What am I looking at?" she asked, squinting at the picture Sloane was pointing at. Unfortunately, she was too short to clearly see it.

"I think some of these pictures are of the house after the robbery!" Sloane whispered excitedly.

Amelia tried hopping up and down to catch glimpses of the picture. She was pretty sure Sloane was right, but it was kind of hard to tell when she could only look at it for about a millionth of a second. Then, inspired, Amelia lifted up her phone to snap a picture of it.

Using her fingers to zoom in on the picture while Sloane peered over her shoulder, Amelia realized that the other girl was definitely right. The black-and-white photograph showed the same room that had been in *Notorious and Illustrious Citizens of Fulton County*. Only in this picture, the wall panel to the right of the fireplace wasn't in one piece anymore. Several police officers stood around, pointing at a gaping hole and the twisted remains of a door upon the floor.

"Here, let me take a picture of the one above it, too." Using her own phone, Sloane took the picture and sent it to Amelia. "It's the same one as in *Notorious and Illustrious Citizens*. The safe was hidden behind a wall panel. When Thomas blew apart the safe, he blew apart the fancy wall panel, too."

Right about then, Amelia's mom came over to them, so Sloane tucked away her phone. Puppet Lady gestured everyone toward the east wing of the house. "This way to your rooms. The gentlemen can change in here. The ladies, in here. The ... *children* ... in there."

She said "children" the way another person might have said "rats" or "cockroaches."

The rooms didn't have regular doors with regular doorknobs on them. Instead, they were made to look like the rest of the wooden paneling in the hallway. You had to know where to push to release the catch.

"They're like secret compartments," Sloane observed.

Puppet Lady gave her an icy smile. "They're original to the house. The millionaire who built this house had very unique tastes."

Amelia didn't say it aloud, but she couldn't help but think that Jacob Hoäl hadn't really built the house. He'd paid people like Thomas to do it.

"Sloane," she whispered. "Didn't one of the books say that Jacob used to build the secret compartments used by the magician in the circus?"

However, before Sloane could reply, the puppet lady shushed them so ferociously that even Slayer Sloane took a step backward.

Everyone went into the rooms Puppet Lady pointed at. She came to Amelia and Sloane's room last of all. There were two leather chairs that looked very comfortable, each with a basin of water for the girls to stick their feet into.

Sloane looked into one in revulsion. Amelia joined her.

"Why are there fish in here?"

Little silvery fish darted about in that excited way fish do when they are about to get fed.

"It's one of our luxury treatments." Puppet Lady stuck her nose up into the air. "They eat the dead skin off your feet."

"They do *what* now?" Sloane demanded, skittering backward against the wall.

"Don't be so childish, child." Puppet Lady sneered. "It's organic, biodegradable, and all natural."

Way to get eaten alive, Amelia finished in her mind, also backing up.

"Your parents have paid for this; now let the fish snack on your feet." Puppet Lady marched out through the hidden panel and slammed it shut afterward.

The fish looked a lot like anchovies.

Anchovies that had ordered a people pizza and were pleased that it had just been delivered.

"Let's get out of here," Sloane said. Amelia nodded her head vigorously in agreement. They wriggled into the robes that had been left for them. Sloane's fit her pretty well, but Amelia was so short that hers dragged on the floor. She had to roll up the sleeves into fat doughnuts around her wrist to keep them from flopping over her hands by several inches. Her slippers were too big also, so she bent to adjust them on her feet.

That was when Amelia noticed the floor.

"Sloane." She tugged at the other girl's arm. "Look!"

The floor was actually a mosaic made out of different types of wood stained all sorts of colors. Together, they formed a circle sliced up like a pie, alternating red-stained wood and gold-stained wood. All around the edges, it was scalloped.

It looked exactly like what a circus tent would look like if you were standing underneath it.

"Those are elephants along the edges." Now it was Sloane's turn to point.

"Thomas *had* to have been the one to do that woodwork, just like you thought!" Amelia said excitedly. "After all, he was the one who was circus obsessed, not Jacob! I bet Jacob didn't even care what things looked like as long as they were fancy and expensive!"

Sloane, however, deflated a bit rather than sharing Amelia's excitement. "I'm not sure how that gets us any closer to the missing jewels, though. I mean, we already knew that Thomas worked at the house."

Fortunately, Amelia had plenty of experience persisting in the face of potential failure. So, she explained, "Don't you see? If these rooms look like secret compartments, then I bet there are *real* secret compartments, too!"

"And Thomas could have hidden the jewels in one, thinking he'd come back to get them once Dr. Barber had taken care of his injures," Sloane said slowly. Warming to the idea, she added, "But Dr. Barber gave him that sleeping syrup stuff that made him pass out, and by the time he woke up, the police were all over the mansion, and he couldn't go back to it!"

"Let's see if we can find this room." Amelia held up her phone to show the picture from the front lobby. "Let's start there and imagine we're Thomas. Maybe if we can retrace how he got out of the house, we can figure out where he might have stuffed the jewels along the way."

Amelia got out an elastic band and used it to fix her phone to her forehead. That made Sloane do a double take.

"*What* are you doing?" the other girl demanded.

"Filming what we're doing, of course." Amelia thought that was pretty obvious.

"That's fine, once we've found the right room. Until then, we're undercover. It's going to be hard enough to wander around the spa without people asking questions *without* a phone strapped to your head. Like some, I dunno, social media unicorn."

"Someday, I bet we'll all be social media unicorns and walk around with phones on our foreheads," Amelia grumbled, but for now she supposed Sloane had a point. Instead, they both wrapped towels around their heads and spread some sort of goo on their faces.

It was just as well that she listened to the other girl. As soon as they stepped out into the hallway they smacked right into Mr. Roth.

And Milton.

And Belinda.

And Principal Stuckey.

Amelia actually knocked Milton over so that the librarian had to catch him in her arms to keep him from falling down.

Yup, he was definitely Hufflepuff, not Gryffindor. Even if he was wearing a scarlet robe with a gold crest on it.

Belinda helped the historian back to his feet as Mr. Roth looked pained.

"What are you doing here?" everyone asked at the same time.

An awkward pause immediately followed.

Then Mr. Roth cleared his throat and said, "Principal Stuckey suggested that I bring Ms. Gomez and Mr. Unserios here for a refreshing spa day to thank them for all that they've done to help the school with this project."

"My treat." Principal Stuckey beamed. "My husband gave me quite a nice gift certificate here, but I'm allergic to nail polish."

"I've never had a pedicure before!" Milton chirped happily. Beneath his robe, he still had on a button-down shirt and bow tie.

Off they went to get that pedicure, while Amelia and Sloane looked at each other uncertainly.

Was it just bad luck that they kept running into those guys? Or was there something more than luck going on here? Could Mr. Roth, Principal Stuckey, Milton, or Belinda be *following* them?

Amelia thought again about the joke she and Sloane had made yesterday. "You don't think they could *really* be using us to find the missing jewels, do you?"

"I dunno. It's been a crazy couple of days. I mean, take this place. What a house of horrors. It's like something out of *Doctor Who*! Hidden panels, women who have obviously been transformed into puppets by some sort of witchcraft, and now getting fed to the fishies. I don't think we can rule out that we're being used by a pack of murderous, scheming adults. On the bright side, maybe we'll luck out and run into the ghost of Thomas Zimmerman. At least he'd be able to tell us what he did with the jewels."

Amelia snickered. "You know, you never talk about stuff like that at school. Just sports."

"Oh. Well." Sloane hesitated, her normal cool missing. "I like science fiction. But only nerds like things like that."

"Not Slayer Sloane."

"Yeah, not Slayer Sloane." For a moment, Sloane looked like she didn't even know who that was. Then she straightened up, thinned out her lips, and said, "Come on. We've got work to do."

They didn't know where Jacob's study was, obviously, but the newspaper article they'd read had mentioned that the study was on the first floor. They just had to open doors until they found a room that looked like the picture out in the front lobby.

The first hidden panel they figured out how to open revealed a woman clutching the armrests of her chair for dear life. A very determined-looking man wielded what might have been a floor sander as he buffed the calluses from the bottom of her feet.

They both stopped what they were doing to look at Amelia and Sloane as though the two girls were the horrific part of the scene.

"Oops. Thought this was the bathroom." Amelia slammed the panel shut. To Sloane, she said, "Your turn to open one."

The room Sloane opened up had a man getting his ear and nostril hair plucked, while the room after that had a woman getting stones laid on her back like it was the seventeenth century and she'd just been accused of witchcraft.

Sloane had been right about this being a house of horrors. Adults spent their money on the weirdest stuff.

Finally, they found the right room. It seemed to be the puppet lady's office but was still recognizable as the room from the picture out in the front lobby.

"Wow," Amelia breathed as she took the towel off her head and used it to wipe the goo from her face. "This is where it all happened. The start of the Hoäl curse."

"The Hoäl curse?" Taking off her disguise too, Sloane gave Amelia a look. "That's not a thing."

"It is now." Amelia switched her camera on and started filming.

Sloane rolled her eyes but didn't argue. She was probably too awestruck by the room to bother. This one didn't just have a wooden floor, it had wood-paneled walls as well. Except they weren't boring square or rectangular panels with lines in between like out in the hallway. These were divided into sections by slender columns made to look like trees. Stylized branches spread out in even patterns to form the tops and bottoms of each panel.

Amelia went over to inspect the spot where the safe had once been, to the right of a fancy marble fireplace. No one must have known how to piece all of that complicated woodwork back together again, so they'd just turned it into a bunch of shelves instead. There were books on it with names like *The Stingy Spa Owner's Guide to Success: Feed Your Pets and Make a Mint!*

Amelia had known those fish were a scam.

Meanwhile, Sloane spotted something that interested her on the opposite side of the fireplace. Whatever it was, it made her cry out "Amelia!" Then, rather than waiting for her to come over, Sloane grabbed Amelia and dragged her to the wall. Hopping up and down excitedly, she pointed at it. "Look! *Look!*"

So, of course Amelia looked.

Carved into the trunks of the trees were various circus performers and animals.

You had to look hard to spot them, but they were there: a roaring lion, a clown juggling, a seal balancing a ball on its nose, the ringmaster in his suit. The trapeze artist, the elephant, the magician—every conceivable circus act.

Thomas had carved these. He had to have. He'd wanted to be a clown—someone who would delight the world. Make them laugh and forget about their troubles for a while. Instead, he'd gotten stuck in a job he hated.

Amelia could relate to that all too well. She was stuck living a life that didn't seem to fit her, either. She too was full of strange and sometimes—she was willing to admit—not great ideas.

She reached her fingers forward to press the clown, to feel the ridges of the wood against her fingertips.

Instead, the shape gave slightly beneath them.

Amelia yelped and jumped back. "Sloane! The clown moved! The clown moved!"

"What clown? Where?" Now Sloane jumped back and looked around wildly. As though expecting to see an ax-wielding maniac spring out at them from somewhere.

"This clown, *here*." Amelia pushed down on the clown again. It visibly moved downward by half an inch but nothing else happened. "I can feel a spring beneath it, I think. Like something is supposed to happen when you press it, but nothing does."

Sloane was far stronger than Amelia, having built up her muscles playing volleyball and softball. She shoved at the clown with all of her might, but nothing happened.

"It's supposed to do something, I'm sure of it," Amelia said, worried that Sloane might think it was just a bit of loose paneling.

However, the other girl had far more imagination than Amelia once would have given her credit for. "I think you're right. And I think it *is* doing something. But I think—maybe—you're supposed to press down on one of the other circus performers too. Like, this undoes one of the panel's latches, but you need to push down on another one as well."

"Do you think this could be it?" Amelia asked excitedly. "Do you?"

"It's definitely *a* secret panel. So, yeah." Sloane chewed her lip. "Thomas knew it was here because he made it. When he got hurt, he probably decided to stuff the jewels in here long enough to go get stitched up by Dr. Barber."

"Only, Dr. Barber gave him that sleeping-syrup stuff that made him pass out for a really long time," Amelia said. "By the time he woke up, there were cops all over the place."

"He couldn't get the jewels back because of that. So, he hopped on the first train to Chicago to . . . I dunno. Either escape or beg his old friend Jacob to forgive him, I guess." Sloane ran her hand over the panel. "The question is, which of these other performers do we need to press down to open up the compartment?"

"That's easy. We just try all of them." Even as Amelia said it, she realized it wouldn't really be that easy after all. There were dozens of circus performers carved into the trunks, boughs, and leaves of the trees. You had to have a bit of an imagination to spot them, too, or you'd never even realize they were there.

Out in the hallway, voices moved toward the office.

"I'm so very sorry that you soiled your robe by dropping your tea on it when some short, hairy person walked in on you unannounced. Let me just..." The puppet lady's voice trailed off as she slid the office panel open and stepped into the room.

Only to jerk to a halt as she spotted the two intruders.

The spa owner was followed by the man who'd been getting his nose hairs plucked, his fluffy white robe no longer white nor fluffy.

They froze and regarded the girls like they were piles of stinky gym socks.

"*What* are you two doing in here?" Puppet Lady demanded.

"Secret compartment," Amelia squeaked.

Sloane sprang into action, shoving their towels into the puppet lady's startled hands. "Our towels need washing too! Thanks! Bye!"

With that, Sloane pushed both Puppet Lady and Nose Hair Man out of the room, slid the door panel shut, and twisted the old-fashioned lock into place.

She turned to Amelia with wild, frantic eyes. "I can't believe I just did that. Is that a crime? I think it might be a crime. I'm going to go to jail with Nanna Tia."

"You are an absolutely brilliant, brave heroine and the poets will sing of your exploits all through time!" Amelia exclaimed, grabbing Sloane by the hand and dragging her back to the secret compartment while the two people on the other side of the door pounded on it, demanding that they open up.

"I have no idea what you're talking about." Sloane wasn't just twisting her hair around her fingers; she was gnawing on it, too. That couldn't be a good sign, but she said, "Okay, if my dad is going to have to pick me up at the police station, then it better be worth it. Let's get this thing open."

"I've got this." Amelia snatched a letter opener off the desk and attacked the panel with it, wedging the tip of the blade into the crack running along the tree trunk. "This happens to my locker all the time. I'll just force it open!"

"Uh, how about if we go with the less drastic option of figuring out what else we need to press down?" Diving forward, Sloane wrenched the letter opener out of her hands.

"Because there isn't time!"

"Amelia?" her mother's voice barked from the other side of the door. "Open up this instant!"

"Oh no." Amelia clasped her hands to her head.

"We've got to keep thinking like Thomas." Sloane closely inspected the carvings, doing a remarkable job of ignoring all of the chaos clamoring against the other side of the office door. No wonder the other kids called her Slayer. "He and Jacob Hoäl ran off to the circus together, right? He wanted to become a clown and Jacob wanted to become—what, exactly?"

"Amelia, you need to open the door right away and come out here to apologize to Mrs. Popanz!" the Judge shouted through the door.

"She probably doesn't know how!" Ashley shouted.

"Don't worry, Amelia! We'll talk you through it!" Aiden cried.

Now Amelia was tugging at her own hair.

"Jacob just managed the circus," she said over the sound of her siblings explaining how to open a door. "What does a circus manager look like?"

"Maybe this guy?" Sloane pointed at the ringmaster in his high boots and tall hat.

"Try it!" But when they did, it didn't budge even a little bit.

An old-fashioned key scratched at the outside of the lock,

while others jangled on a key ring. Through the wood, Puppet Lady muttered, "No, it's not that one. I think it's this—no, it's not that one, either."

"Maybe he wanted to be a magician! No—maybe the lion tamer? No . . ." Now Sloane was just randomly jabbing at the figures hidden in the trees. Or even anything that looked remotely like a figure, given that some of them could be terribly hard to pick out. In fact, that figure over there looked like he was practically fading away. Like he was trying to creep behind a tree and slip away from the rest of them . . .

"That one!" Amelia gasped, pointing. "The clown was Thomas, and that's Jacob! *Creeping off and leaving the circus behind.*"

The key turned in the old-fashioned lock with a heavy *CLUNK*. The door itself fell open, and a large number of very angry and excited people tumbled through it.

Ignoring them all, Sloane pushed at the retreating figure.

The wood wiggled beneath her fingers.

Within the wall, something groaned like it had rusted.

"*What* do the two of you think you're doing?" Amanda Poe demanded over the chorus of her husband, daughter, and stepson, all of whom were offering their opinions about what Amelia and Sloane were doing.

Meanwhile, Mr. Roth looked like he was considering retirement.

Principal Stuckey looked pained.

Milton looked confused.

The puppet lady looked like she was thinking about cutting out the fish and just eating Amelia and Sloane herself.

Nose Hair Man looked about like what you would expect someone to look like if they'd been having their nostril hairs plucked.

Only Belinda looked respectfully approving. "Working together to fight the system? Righteous, man."

Amelia and Sloane still had the figures pressed down and could feel something inside the wall grinding away, trying to open.

Rather than answering her mother, Amelia banged her fist against the panel to pop it open.

Sometimes she had to do that with her locker, too.

Serendipitously, the door finally sprang open.

Less luckily, the door knocked Amelia to the floor as it did so.

Everyone else in the room rushed forward to get a good look. Only her mom and dad paused long enough to bend down and give her a hand up.

By the time she got to her feet, everyone else was gasping in shock—and disappointment.

Disappointment?

What was there to be disappointed about? There had to be a whole heap of jewels inside the secret compartment!

Pushing her way forward as Sloane detached herself from the group, Amelia finally saw what everyone else saw:

Nothing but dust.

And an old-fashioned, peaked clown hat.

Zemblanity.

7

A New Lead and a New Threat

Finding an empty secret compartment wasn't nearly as exciting as finding a treasure trove of missing jewels. Still, it was enough to get Sloane and Amelia featured on WTOL's five-o'clock news show and for the *Fulton County Expositor* to send out a reporter to interview them.

Little did they know it, but the person who'd set this project into motion was not pleased with this turn of events. For that person, watching the report on the news was not serendipitous. It was most definitely zemblanitatious. This person wanted the seventh-grade students of Wauseon Middle School to collect leads. Not get everyone in northwest Ohio interested in finding a long-forgotten fortune in missing jewels.

However, one person's bad luck was another person's good luck. Amelia was in heaven, preening for the camera with that weird clown hat on her head and launching into a long speech about how they'd made the discovery. Sloane got the feeling this might be the only time Amelia had ever gotten to talk this much in front of her family without one of them interrupting her. However, the Miller-Poes weren't being interviewed by the TV news crew and Amelia was. They had no choice but to remain silent.

Unlike her partner, Sloane endured it all with gritted teeth.

What she really wanted to do was talk to Amelia alone. With all of those blathering adults around, she never got the chance.

Which was unfortunate. Because the secret compartment had not, in fact, been empty aside from that hat.

There'd also been a postcard in it.

Sloane had been both quick enough and lucky enough to snatch it up and tuck it into her robe before anyone else saw it. She'd figured that the adults would hijack their discovery, and she'd been right.

No matter how hard she tried, though, she couldn't drag Amelia out of the spotlight. The other girl was drinking up the attention, and Sloane wasn't sure she'd ever stop. Amelia would probably mug one of the cameramen, steal his camera, and keep on broadcasting all night long. Whereas Sloane escaped gratefully with her dad as soon as she could.

Both of Sloane's grannies (though not her great-granny Nanna Tia, who was busy sweet-talking the local sheriff into believing that she was just a harmless little old lady and not an illegal bingo czarina) were waiting for her in the kitchen when her dad proudly ushered her in through the door.

"There she is, our Sloane-y!" They enveloped Sloane in a cloud of kisses, pats, and cheek-pinches.

For about the tenth time, Dad joked, "Slayer Sloane slaying it on TV!"

"Daaaaaad," Sloane groaned, also for about the tenth time. Then she noticed something beyond her grannies. "Wait. There are countertops. When did that happen?"

The counters were no longer made of plywood. Instead, her

dad had installed the butcher block countertops just like her mom had always wanted. The wood had been sitting in a stack at the back of the eating nook for the last three years.

"While you were off making amazing discoveries with your friend Amelia!" Granny Pearl pinched her son's cheek.

"Maisy would be so proud of these!" Granny Kitty patted her son-in-law's other cheek.

Sloane expected her dad to say how great the counters were, but he didn't.

He just kept smiling. A real smile.

Sloane didn't know what to make of that.

"Do you think Dad's all right?" she asked Granny Kitty later that evening as she helped Sloane take her clean laundry up to her room. "It's just . . . he's fixing the house up and he smiled earlier without saying how great everything is. He hasn't really done either one of those things since he had Mom to do them with."

"Oh, Sloane-y." Granny Kitty hesitated and took the laundry basket from Sloane's hands. "I think maybe your dad is finally . . . moving on."

"Moving *on*?" It was just as well that Granny Kitty had taken the basket. If Sloane had still been holding it, she would have dropped the clean laundry all over the floor. "What does that mean?"

Granny Kitty's face softened. "I miss my Maisy too, Sloane, and I always will. But your father has to live his life. Just like you're living yours, having adventures with your friend Amelia."

"She's not my friend," Sloane corrected automatically.

Only to realize that might be a lie. Amelia actually felt like her friend. A real friend.

In a way that Mackenzie, Kylee, and Mylie weren't.

Granny Kitty might think that Sloane was living her life, but her granny was wrong. She was living Slayer Sloane's life, and Slayer Sloane was friends with people like Mackenzie, Kylee, and Mylie. Not weirdos like Amelia.

However, maybe Sloane Actually Living Her Life *was* friends with Amelia.

Her mom would like Amelia way better than she did any of Sloane's volleyball friends. Not that she didn't like them.

But Sloane could hear her mom's voice in her head. *You can be yourself with Amelia.*

After Granny Kitty went back downstairs, Sloane curled up on the window seat in her bedroom and pulled up Amelia's YouTube channel. What do you know? After her TV interview, Amelia now had close to fifty followers. Sloane wasn't super thrilled that Amelia was already posting the videos she'd created about the case. Now other kids could steal their ideas.

More creepily still, it occurred to Sloane that there was no way to know who those people really were. She scrolled through their usernames, but she didn't recognize any of them from school. Even if she'd come across someone like "MacAttackS," how would she really know it was Mackenzie? What if their joke yesterday, about someone using the seventh grade to find the treasure, had been truer than they realized?

If so, Amelia was making it awfully easy for that person.

Telling herself not to be so dramatic, Sloane took out the postcard she'd stolen from the safe. On the front, it had a black-and-white photo of a tallish, oldish building. Someone had added color to it, along with the words:

Hotel Waldorf
Toledo, Ohio

Flipping it over, Sloane discovered that someone had scrawled a message across the back:

Find the baby, find the jewels.

Sloane almost took a picture of it to send to Amelia. Then it occurred to her that one of the other Miller-Poes might see it. The last thing Amelia needed was for her family to offer more opinions on their project.

Setting aside her phone, Sloane googled "Hotel Waldorf Toledo." Apparently it had been a hotel along the river in downtown Toledo between 1916 and 1979. It had been pretty fancy, too, with a rooftop garden and a front desk made out of a solid chunk of marble. Sloane imagined you'd have to be pretty rich to stay there.

Which of course you would be if you'd just stolen a bunch of jewels.

Except that Thomas Zimmerman hadn't lived long enough to sell the jewels, let alone stay at a fancy hotel. He'd died in the train crash all the way back in 1887. Whoever had left this note behind had done so *at least* thirty years later. Maybe more than that. There were cars in this picture, and Sloane didn't think that they were the right kind for 1916.

So . . . *had* the jewels ever been in that secret compartment? Sloane sort of thought they had to have been. At least for a while. Then, just like Sloane and Amelia, someone else had figured out they were there and stolen them all over again. Someone who had left behind a message for . . . who? Thomas?

Was it possible that he hadn't died in the train collision after all?

Only, if that was the case, why hadn't *he* removed the jewels from the secret compartment years before 1916 or whenever?

And who was the baby? By 1916, it couldn't be Jacob's son, Charles. He'd have been all grown up by then. And who was doing the writing? And to whom?

Sloane needed Amelia's thoughts on these questions. Amelia looked at things the way no one else did, came up with solutions that no one else would dream of. Like breaking into a museum. And a spa.

Giving up, Sloane went to sleep, eager for once for the school week to start. In the morning, she got up early, dressed in a hurry, and flew out the kitchen door. Her dad gave her a groggy kiss as he shuffled about, coffee cup in hand. He managed to mumble, "See you after school. Love you!"

"Same!" Sloane blew him a kiss.

She rode her bike across town to school. Near her locker, she found Kylee and Mylie talking excitedly about Amelia and Sloane appearing on the news.

"Wow! The two of you are the team to beat!" Mylie grinned.

"Amelia sounded so smart when that reporter was interviewing her!" Kylee said in awe. "I would have been, like, too embarrassed to talk!"

Mackenzie stood sulkily off to the side. She looked very much like someone had shoved an entire lemon into her mouth.

It occurred to Sloane that it was probably upsetting Mackenzie's world to discover Amelia was the source of so much respectful interest. Because if Amelia could go *up* in the world, then that meant that Mackenzie could go *down*.

Trying to right things, Mackenzie giggled disdainfully and then sneered, "Leave it to the Yeti to do something cringey and not be embarrassed by it!"

There were close to a dozen kids gathered around, listening. At this, they all laughed too, snapping back into their old habit of taking cues from Mackenzie.

Sloane didn't laugh.

It would have been the easier thing to do.

But when you'd plotted to break into a museum, and ransacked a spa together, it made a bond. So instead, she said, "*Yeti*, Mackenzie? That name is, like, *so over*. I can't believe you're still using it."

That made everyone stop and look at each other uncertainly. Was it lame now to call Amelia "Yeti"? If so, when had that happened? Would they get made fun of for using it? *Might they be the next yeti if they did?*

Feeling her power shifting, Mackenzie switched into Mac

Attack mode. "Oh, and when did that happen? When the Yeti became your partner?"

"No, when it became boring," Sloane shot back.

To her surprise, Kylee jumped in. "Yeah, I'm kinda done with the yeti thing too. I can't even remember how it all started, but it just seems sort of old now."

Of course, Amelia chose that moment to walk down the hallway dressed like a movie star.

At least, Sloane had to assume that was what the other girl had been going for. Amelia wore a floor-length black dress, heels, a pair of oversized sunglasses, and a coat flung over her shoulders.

"I'll sign autographs at lunch," she announced grandly. "But no selfies without permission from my publicist."

Mackenzie smirked at Sloane, who wondered if it was possible to melt into the floor and disappear forever. She hustled over to Amelia and greeted her like it was the most natural thing in the world to show up in class wearing your sister's old prom dress. "Amelia! Buddy! Great dress! Uh, can I talk to you?"

She dragged her partner over to the far corner of Mr. Roth's room, by the reading area and bookshelves.

"Why are you dressed like that?" Sloane hissed.

Amelia's skin flamed bright red, but she crossed her arms and shot right back, "Why are *you* dressed like *that*?"

Sloane glanced downward to confirm that she was, in fact, still wearing jeans and a hoodie. "What do you mean? I always dress like this."

"Exactly! This is one of the most momentous days of our lives, and you look like everyone else! Don't you want to be unique?"

"No! I want to be . . ." Sloane trailed off. She'd been about to say *I want to be exactly like everyone else*. But confronted with Amelia's too-bright eyes, Sloane realized that was a big fat lie.

She didn't want to be like everyone else. It just seemed smarter to camouflage herself among them until it was safe to actually be herself. Probably sometime in her thirties.

"Look, who cares what I want to be? I've got something important to tell you."

Since Mackenzie had come into the room and was eyeing them, Sloane turned her back and dropped her voice lower as she told Amelia all about what she'd found. Even though they weren't supposed to have their phones out in class, she pulled up a picture of the note.

"WHAT?! That's the most amazing—*GUHMUPH!*"

Sloane clapped her hand over the other girl's mouth, warning, "We don't want anyone else to know!"

Pushing Sloane's hand away, Amelia hissed, "Why not? We'd probably get back on the news again! The number of subscribers to my YouTube channel has already gone from eight to fifty!"

"Yeah, well, think of how many you'll get if we actually *find* the jewels. Which we might not be able to do if everyone else has the same clues."

Amelia's eyes got so big that Sloane was pretty sure she could actually see through them to the wheels turning in the girl's head. But before Amelia could respond, the day's guests arrived and class began. First Mr. Roth proudly told the class about what Amelia and

Sloane had discovered. Then they all had a chance to take turns speaking with the local history experts stationed around the room.

Since Mackenzie was still watching them with laser-beam eyes, Sloane hustled Amelia over to a wizened old man in a green shirt. Mr. Roth had said he was ninety years old, and he looked every day of it. He was so tiny that he and Amelia were practically the same height. With that emerald shirt, he looked like a leprechaun. Sparse hair waved about his spotted head, but his eyes were bright and clear, and when Sloane introduced herself, he bellowed back, "NAME'S TIMOTHY NEIKIRK! I'M AN AUCTIONEER!"

Sloane and Amelia took a step backward.

Realizing he was yelling, he handed them a card and said in a quieter voice, "Heh. Sorry about that! Sometimes I get so used to auctioning things off that I forget to speak in my regular voice. So, who'll give me one-dolla, one-dolla, one-dolla for information on the Hoäl case? Do I have one-dolla, one-dolla, one-dolla—oops! There I go again, heh-heh-heh."

Sloane was fairly certain that Timothy Neikirk would have, in fact, forced them to pay one dollar to find out what he knew. Except Mr. Roth's head whipped around right then, his eyes narrowing in a way that would have made both Belinda and Mackenzie proud.

"I hear you found Thomas Zimmerman's old hat. Want to hear about his time as a circus clown?" the auctioneer asked cheerfully.

"Definitely not." Sloane shuddered.

"How about how Jacob Hoäl increased his millions by marrying a wealthy widower?"

"No," Sloane said, just as Amelia clasped her hands together and gasped, "Oh, *yes*! I bet it was a love match! *Say* it was a love match! Say that they looked into each other's eyes and immediately knew it was true love."

"Nope! She was about as sour as they came!" Mr. Neikirk pulled out an old photo on stiff sepia-toned cardboard. It showed a very pretty woman with a twisted mouth and a nose held like she was sniffing something bad. She wore a diamond necklace so big it practically covered her entire chest. Jacob stood behind her, his hand on her shoulder. "Very strict! Didn't believe in dancing, singing, playing cards—"

"Sounds just like the Hoäl family," Amelia interjected.

"Yes, in-deedy!" The auctioneer beamed. "You've done your homework, missy!"

"It's Amelia, actually, not 'missy.' And yes, I *always* do my homework." Amelia clasped her hands together and looked angelic.

Sloane rolled her eyes. Amelia might be many things, but a dedicated student was not one of them.

"Hey, are those some of the jewels that Thomas stole?" Sloane asked, pointing at the ugly necklace Lucretia was wearing.

"Yup! That necklace cost Jacob fifty thousand dollars. That would be over a million dollars these days."

"Yeah, that's great." Sloane figured she'd better get down to business. Mackenzie was inching her way toward them. "Hey, you don't know what happened to the baby, do you?"

"Which one?" Mr. Neikirk asked, leaning on his cane.

That pulled Sloane up short. Amelia, too, by the look of her. The two girls exchanged a glance. Amelia said, "What, now?"

"I said, which baby did you want to know about?"

"There's more than one baby in this story?" Sloane asked.

"Course there is! You didn't know that?" The auctioneer looked from one to the other of them while they shook their heads.

"We only know about Charles Hoäl," Amelia said.

"Ah, but Thomas Zimmerman had a son, too. That's why he robbed the Hoäls in the first place. He'd just gotten married and had a baby. Needed the money to support his family."

Terrific.

They didn't have just one century-old baby to find. They had two.

Of all the luck.

"I don't even *like* babies," Amelia said morosely over lunch. The two of them were sitting together at a table as far away from everyone else as they could get. Normally Sloane sat with a bunch of the other athletes and Amelia sat by herself. If Sloane was honest with herself, this was sort of a nice break from being piled up with a bunch of stinky, competitive kids. Last week, one of the football players had brought what he said was a ghost pepper for everyone to try, if they were brave enough. While Sloane was pretty sure it hadn't been an actual ghost pepper, her mouth had still been on fire two class periods later.

"It's not like we're finding a baby we have to keep and raise," Sloane pointed out. "These babies grew up, grew old, and died a long time ago. I guess we just have to find out what happened to them both and that will . . ."

Sloane trailed off because she had no idea how to end that sentence. She toyed with a sweet potato tater tot.

"Who do you think took the treasure, anyhow?" Amelia asked,

poking at the salad she'd brought in from home with her fork. "Do you think Thomas could have faked his own death?"

"Doubt it, but I guess we could ask Milton what he thinks."

"Oh! Unless Thomas left it as a clue for Jacob, knowing that he'd check the other secret compartment!"

"That doesn't work. That card got left there *at least* thirty years after Jacob definitely died in the train crash. Probably even more than that." Sloane stared at the tater tot in her fingers. "I feel kinda bad for Thomas now that I know he wanted the money for his family."

According to the leprechaun—er, Mr. Neikirk—Thomas's wife, Beatrice, had had a baby the week before the robbery. They had been living in a really horrible, tiny log cabin that had been old and gross even by the standards of a hundred and thirty years ago.

Amelia gave up on her salad and lay down her fork. "Hey, do you think Beatrice could have left the note? No, never mind. She never knew what happened to the jewels."

At Milton's station, he'd explained to everyone that the townspeople at the time had thought Thomas must have given Beatrice the jewels. However, she'd spent the rest of her life living with her sister's family because she didn't have much money.

"Maybe she just pretended that she didn't have any money until people forgot about her." Sloane threw the tater tot into the garbage can stationed in the middle of the cafeteria floor. One of the lunch ladies whipped her head around, so Sloane immediately shoved her nose in her Chromebook.

"But they never did, and the memory of Thomas's crimes pursued her to the ends of the earth—and to the end of her life." Amelia stood up theatrically and laid her hand on her heart. "Yet still she loved him, for no matter how dastardly or foul his deeds, they were soul mates, destined to—"

Grabbing Amelia by the arm, Sloane pulled her down into her seat again. "Destined to draw *too much attention to themselves.*"

"Yeah, well, I stand by my soul-mate theory." Amelia crossed her arms grumpily.

"Fine. Just don't stand while you're standing by it, okay?"

Across the cafeteria, Mackenzie stared at them with that look she got right before she spiked the ball and obliterated someone on the opposing team.

While that attitude was a great thing to have in a teammate, it was less great to have in an opponent. With a sinking feeling, Sloane realized that Mackenzie probably now viewed *her* as an opponent.

This theory was confirmed when Sloane went into the bathroom without Amelia right after lunch. Mackenzie followed her in and gave a death glare to the only other girl in there, Taylor Villarreal. Who had made the mistake of wanting to wash her hands after using the toilet.

Taylor immediately withered beneath Mackenzie's death stare and ran from the room.

Hopefully she had some hand sanitizer in her locker.

"You and the Yeti are suddenly good friends," Mackenzie

said oh-so-casually as she went to the mirror to adjust the ridiculously huge bow holding her ponytail in place.

"Don't call her that."

"What? Yeti?" Smiling, Mackenzie turned around. "Why not? I thought you loved that name. After all, *you're the one who gave it to her.*"

Oh no.

Oh no, no, no, no, *no.*

Everyone had forgotten that Sloane had started that name. Probably because Sloane had only ever said it the one time. It was everyone else who had spread it around, not her.

Leave it to Mac Attack Snyder to remember an incriminating detail.

"How do you think your new bestie would feel if she found out that *you* were the one who came up with her favorite nickname?" Mackenzie circled Sloane slowly, a lion toying with its food.

Sloane wasn't about to be anyone's meal, however. "Why do you even care, Mac? What's it to you?"

"What it is to me is that I want to get an A on this project, and I'm matched up with dumb Drake, who thinks we should just say the butler did it and go play video games." Mackenzie narrowed her eyes while Sloane's heart sank. "What *I* want is information, and you two seem to be pretty good at finding it. What *I* want is to know everything you find out about the missing jewels. Text me as soon as you know anything, and I won't tell Amelia the truth."

Sloane's heart beat double-time. Like it wanted to bust right out of her rib cage to pummel Mackenzie over the head. "We probably won't find out anything else new, you know."

"I do know." Mackenzie smiled slowly, smugly. "Which is why Amelia will probably soon know everything I know too."

With that, she sashayed right out of the bathroom, hair bow ridiculously, triumphantly high.

Sloane shut herself into one of the stalls while her fingers strangled themselves with her hair.

If they didn't find out anything more about the missing treasure, Amelia would know that Sloane was to blame for so much of her suffering this past month.

And if they *did* find out anything else and she told Mackenzie, Sloane would have to betray her new friend all over again.

She wished her mom was here. Maisy Osburn would have listened to her daughter and known what to do. Sloane supposed she could ask her dad, but then he'd worry about her. And if he started to worry, then they wouldn't be able to pretend that things were great anymore. Without that, Sloane didn't know what their lives would look like. She just knew she didn't want the creeping gray mist to ever return.

So, what was she going to do?

No matter which way you looked at it, any good luck she had was going to turn into bad luck.

She might as well not have any luck at all.

8

The Cost of Knowledge

Blissfully unaware of Sloane's dilemma, it fell to Amelia to hunt down Mr. Neikirk after school. She and Sloane realized they'd been so thrown by his revelation that *two* babies had lost parents as a result of Thomas's theft that they'd forgotten to ask him any real questions. Unfortunately, Sloane had softball practice, so Amelia had agreed to go ask him their list of questions.

First, though, she had to go home and change. The high heels she'd worn to school were killing her ankles. No wonder they called them "stilettos." That was a kind of knife, which was exactly what it felt like someone was jabbing into her feet and legs.

There was a package on the front step, and to Amelia's surprise, it was addressed to her. She didn't think she'd ever received a package before. Sometimes Grandma Suzy still sent her cards on holidays, but there weren't any holidays coming up. Plus, Grandma Suzy always hand-wrote the addresses on her cards, and this one had been printed out.

It was a box, had Amelia only known it, that would take her one step closer to being attacked by a slingshot-carrying would-be thief. If she'd never opened it, she probably wouldn't have ended up getting a concussion from an unlucky acorn aimed right at her head.

Of course, if Amelia had known any of that, she'd probably have opened it anyhow.

(She would, however, have worn a helmet to the cemetery later that week.)

Amelia set the box aside, though she was insanely curious about what was in it. Maybe one of her forty-two new YouTube followers had sent her fan mail! Unfortunately, she was running on a really tight schedule as tonight was Miller-Poe Tennis Night. Before that nightmare took place, Amelia needed to track down Mr. Neikirk and shake as much information as she could out of him for as little as possible. At school, he'd actually auctioned off his knowledge to the highest bidder every time Mr. Roth's back was turned.

Amelia reluctantly set the package aside for later and focused on finding Mr. Neikirk. Not only did she want to find out what he had to say, she didn't want to let Sloane down. The few days they'd been working together had been the best of Amelia's life. In fact, she was so happy, that Amelia sort of hoped that she and Sloane wouldn't have the Mystery of the Vanished Hoäl Fortune solved by the time their project for Mr. Roth was due. That way, they'd be able to keep on hanging out together. Which they would, because Amelia knew that there was just no way someone as competitive as Slayer Sloane was going to give up. Not after they'd already uncovered so much more than anyone else had in over a hundred years.

Or . . . better still, they'd solve the Quandary of the Lost Jewels (Amelia still hadn't settled on a name) before they turned in the project. Then she and Sloane would keep on hanging out because they were friends.

Just the thought of it filled Amelia with a glow of happiness. Or better to say that it made that glow burn all the brighter. Because ever since they'd declared a truce after breaking into the Fulton County Historical Museum, Amelia had finally discovered what it felt like to be liked. To have just one single person be on her side.

It felt wonderful.

Gloriously, amazingly wonderful.

As Amelia dug through her closet for the proper outfit to wear to interview Mr. Neikirk, her imagination spun out a lovely future for her. Even after they solved the Puzzle of the Purloined Pearls (no one had mentioned any pearls, but Amelia bet there were some in there somewhere), she and Sloane would continue to investigate mysteries together. In a town as old as Wauseon, there had to be all sorts of secrets and riddles people had never solved. It could be like an after-school job.

Osburn and Poe Detective Agency!

Amelia could film all of their investigations, and turn them into an award-winning documentary series for Netflix!

Suddenly, Amelia realized she was so dazzled by the thought of it that she'd stopped sorting through her clothes from Goodwill at the back of her closet. A glance at her phone told her she'd been doing little more than clutching a jacket and smiling dreamily at the wall for almost ten minutes now.

Yikes. Amelia didn't want to get so caught up in the future that she let her new friend down right now.

Hurrying up, she dug out a suit that she'd found at the thrift store that she felt made her look *exactly* like Eva Marie Saint in *North by Northwest*. That one wasn't a silent movie, but Grandma

Suzy loved it just the same. However, unlike Eva Marie Saint, Amelia paired it with Converse Chucks. She'd had enough of this high-heeled nonsense.

Grabbing a notebook and pen, Amelia found Mr. Neikirk by calling his office: Neikirk Auctioneering, Estate Sales, and Real Estate. It turned out he was pricing stuff for an estate sale at a house near where Sloane lived.

Since Ashley had just gotten home from her job interning at the courthouse, Amelia asked her big sister for a ride.

"What's an estate sale?" Ashley asked as she drove Amelia there.

It took Amelia a long moment to realize her sister was asking her. In fact, Amelia first turned around to confirm that one of her sister's friends wasn't sitting in the back seat. Or a ghost, though what a ghost would be doing haunting the back seat of their car, Amelia didn't know.

It just seemed like a more reasonable explanation than anyone in her family actually asking her anything.

"An estate sale is when someone dies and you sell all their stuff," Amelia said finally.

"Like a dead person garage sale?"

"Pretty much, yeah."

Ashley nodded thoughtfully at that. Amelia waited for her sister to tell her all about dead people and how you got them to give you the best deals on their stuff, but Ashley just kept driving.

Unable to help herself, Amelia said, "Did you just ask me a question? About estate sales?"

"Well, yeah." Her sister looked at Amelia in confusion.

"Because you've never once in my entire life asked me to explain something to you. Not once."

"Oh, that can't be right. I mean, I'm sure I've asked you something like 'Where's the peanut butter?'"

"No." Amelia crossed her arms. "The other day, you actually told me that the peanut butter was in my hand because you weren't sure that I knew that it was there."

"Oh." Ashley blinked rapidly as she pulled to a halt in front of a two-story yellow Victorian with a cupola. "I guess it's just that you seem like you know what you're doing with this project. I was pretty impressed that you and Sloane figured out there was a secret compartment in the old Hoäl mansion."

No one in her family had ever been impressed by anything Amelia had done. Not once. Ever.

However, Amelia felt she could get used to them doing it again. Frequently.

Preening, she got out of the car and snapped open her selfie stick.

"Have I really never asked you a question before?" Ashley called through the open car window as Amelia marched along the garden's stone walkway.

"No, but that makes twice now!" Wow. A real friend *and* respect from her family! Amelia couldn't believe how much better her life had gotten since she'd started hanging out with Sloane.

"Huh." For a moment, Ashley appeared so unsure of herself that she looked completely unlike Amelia's sister. Then she snapped back to her old, confident self and said, "I'll be back in half an hour to pick you up for tennis!" and peeled off down Oak Street, back toward home.

Amelia's elation at finally being taken seriously lasted about five minutes in the company of Mr. Neikirk. Even at ninety years of age, he was still clearly calling the shots in his auction, real estate, and estate sale business. When Amelia walked through the door, he was bossing around half a dozen harried workers. All of them scurried about with Sharpie markers and tape dots.

"MEREDITH, DON'T PUT A PRICE ON THAT! IT'S GOING TO THE AUCTION HOUSE!" he bellowed, jabbing his cane at a woman carrying a large porcelain figurine of a dog. To a man struggling along with an overstuffed chair, he boomed, "NO, NO, NO! TY, THAT STAYS HERE FOR THE ESTATE SALE!"

Ty made a small sound of distress and then swung the chair back around, almost knocking over Meredith and her porcelain dog.

"Granddad, you're using your auctioneer's voice again." Meredith ducked under the chair.

"WHAT? Oh, sorry. Heh-heh-heh." Spotting Amelia, the tiny auctioneer with the enormous voice hopped up from behind the card table he'd been using as a makeshift desk. He hobbled over to see her and cried, "Why, it's the smart missy from school!"

"Nope, it's still Amelia," Amelia corrected. She already had to deal with people calling her "Yeti." She wasn't going to add "missy" to the list of things she wasn't.

"Meredith! Ty! This is one of the little girls who found out more about the missing Hoäl jewels in one weekend than anyone else has discovered in over a hundred years!" Mr. Neikirk pointed proudly at Amelia. Though it was doubtful that Ty could actually see her around that enormous chair. All she could see of him was a pair of buckling knees.

"I'm not actually a little girl," Amelia corrected again. "But thank you for the compliment just the same."

Mr. Neikirk spotted the selfie stick in Amelia's hand. "Hey, what's that, now? Is that one of them camera things? Are you FaceChatting me?"

"Something like that. I've got a YouTube channel," Amelia said proudly. "If you don't mind, I have a few more questions I'd like to ask you."

A glint sprang into the auctioneer's eye at that. "So . . . if you record me in here, the people watching your YouTalk will see what's for sale?"

"I suppose so."

"Excellent!" Mr. Niekerk clapped his hands together and dragged Amelia over in front of an absolutely enormous hall clock. "Scoot to the side there, young lady, and ask me your questions!"

As he nudged Amelia, she realized he'd positioned his head right next to a sticker that read $10,000.

Flabbergasted, Amelia couldn't help but ask, "Does that clock actually cost *ten thousand dollars*?"

"Worth every penny! And it's a steal, at that!" Mr. Neikirk

snapped before tugging Amelia closer and hissing, "Look, you don't tell me how to sell antiques and I won't tell you how to film a movie!"

Straightening back up, he fixed his tie and waited for Amelia's questions.

"Er, well. Um. You said earlier today that there were two babies. What can you tell me about both of them?"

"Ah, well, not much about Jacob's boy, Charles, to be honest with you. I'm afraid that, unlike this clock, which has sat in this exact spot since it was shipped over from Switzerland one hundred and fifty years ago, he did not remain in Wauseon." The auctioneer stepped back so that Amelia's camera could capture more of the clock.

"Uh, Mr. Neikirk," she began, only to be cut off.

"No, Charles's life was much closer to this authentic Tiffany glass lamp over here." Before Amelia could stop him, Mr. Niekerk hurried into the front parlor. "Just as Charles was born into a life of luxury only to be uprooted from his first home and sent on to another before finally returning to Fulton County in his later years, this lamp has traveled too! And much like how the Hoäls' jewels were stolen, this lamp is a steal at a mere five thousand dollars."

"Uh, Mr. Niekerk . . ." Amelia pursed her lips, eyes narrowing. "Maybe you could give me more details about Charles and less about the antiques. . . ."

"Oh, certainly, certainly!" The auctioneer bobbed his head— and then inched toward a marble table. "My grandfather—who took care of the Hoäl estate—said that Charles was sent to live with Lucretia's parents, the Forrests, over in Toledo. Wealthy people but not very much fun, Grandpa said. Considering that *he* wasn't exactly a whole lot of fun, I can only imagine how strict and stern *they* must have been. Still, I'm sure they loved him as best as they knew how. Just like whoever ends up with this Roseville vase will love the fact that they snatched up this rare pattern for a mere eight hundred dollars!"

Desperate to get the auctioneer to focus on her questions, Amelia said, "Mr. Niekerk, you know that my film won't be ready for another week, right?"

That caught him off guard. "What's that, now?"

"Our class project isn't due until next Monday," Amelia confessed. She didn't add that her channel only had about fifty followers anyhow.

"Oh. Well, then. Nothing personal, Miss Amelia, but I've got a business to run." Turning around, Mr. Neikirk returned to slapping labels on things.

Amelia felt like everything was falling apart and she didn't understand why. He'd barely answered any of her questions and Ashley would be picking her up soon. Worse still, she couldn't shake the desperate feeling that she was letting her new friend down. Sloane would be much better at handling Mr. Neikirk than she was. No doubt, Slayer Sloane would stare him down with that cool look of hers, freezing him in place. Instead, the Yeti had been chasing him all over the ground floor of the house without getting much out of him.

Well, she wasn't some weird yeti and she wasn't ready to give up yet. Amelia shoved herself between the auctioneer and a picture he was about to tag. The sticker ended up on her forehead instead.

Peeling it off, Amelia discovered she was worth a mere ten dollars.

While she stood there, temporarily frozen in outrage, the auctioneer escaped into the kitchen through a swinging door, like an evil leprechaun.

That was it. She wasn't letting Sloane down for anything. Amelia was getting something useful out of Mr. Neikirk if she had to threaten to shove her selfie stick up his nostril.

Brandishing her selfie stick, Amelia marched into the kitchen, demanding, "What about the other baby? Thomas's baby? Do you know anything about him? And what about Charles? I know he came back here right before he died. Do you know anything about that?"

Surprised, Mr. Neikirk turned around with a clipboard in his hands. Before he could answer, however, Ty came up out of the basement carrying a very big and very dusty cardboard box. "What about these, boss? It's a crazy-old projector and some home movies from the thirties, I think."

The auctioneer looked pained as he yanked the box down and stood up on his tiptoes so he could peer inside. "'Crazy old' is a term we try not to use in the estate sale business. As for this, it's a bunch of rubbish. Maybe donate it to the historical society, I suppose."

Spotting an opportunity, Amelia pulled out her purse. "I'll give you twenty dollars for the box."

"Really?" Ty sneezed.

"Really?" Mr. Neikirk rubbed his hands together gleefully.

But when he reached for the money, Amelia refused to let it go. "Yes, but this money buys me some answers, too."

Looking back on it, she probably should have just bribed him in the first place.

Mr. Neikirk scowled, but when she wouldn't let the twenty go he said, "Don't know why Charles came back, exactly. He tried turning the Hoäl mansion into apartments right before World War Two, but died soon after. Had the gall to have Whalen's Auctioneers sell the place instead of Grandpa. As for Thomas, he didn't have much of an estate, so Grandpa didn't really know them. That's about all he ever told me, except that the boy had a pretty rough time of it growing up. Back then, people thought if your parents were bad, you must be bad too. If you want to hear more about the Zimmerman baby, I'd talk to Norma Cooke. Beatrice was Norma's great-aunt, and she moved in with the family after Thomas died."

He tried to jerk the twenty-dollar bill away, but Amelia squeezed her fist tighter. "Any idea where Norma Cooke lives?"

"Haven't a clue, but she has a stand at the farmers' market over on Fulton Street on Monday nights. If you leave now, you should still be able to catch her."

Oh, darn. It sounded like she'd have to miss tennis night with her family. What a shame!

Amelia let go of her money, and the auctioneer triumphantly tucked it into a cash box. Ty happily shoved the grubby box into her hands. Staggering beneath its weight, Amelia went out to the curb to find Ashley already waiting for her.

"Holy cow. What did you buy?" Ashley surveyed the dusty box with disgust.

"Cooperation," Amelia said morosely as she dropped the box into Ashley's big, sparkling trunk. "It was more expensive than I thought it was going to be. Hey, I need to skip out on tennis because I have to go to the farmers' market to talk to someone else."

Ashley, however, snagged Amelia by the collar as she attempted to walk off. "Nope. Uh-uh. Nothing doing. It's Miller-Poe Tennis Night and that means *all* Miller-Poes!"

"But—but—but—schoolwork!" Amelia protested as her sister coerced her into the car. At least she got pushed into the front seat instead of the trunk.

"Schoolwork *is* important, but so is your health! A strong body leads to a strong mind and . . ." Ashley continued to lecture her, but Amelia tuned her out. She tried desperately to come up with an argument that would convince her parents to let her go shake down an old lady for information rather than cringe and try to figure out what she was supposed to do with her racket every time someone whacked a ball at her.

(Tennis always made Amelia feel as though she was being executed by a firing squad armed with tennis balls.)

Failing to come up with a convincing argument, she arrived home, only to be stuffed into a ridiculous pleated white skirt and handed a tennis racket.

So much for feeling respected by her family.

At least Sloane was still her friend.

As the Miller-Poe family SUV careened toward the tennis courts and a hideous evening of being forced to do something she both hated and was bad at, Amelia pulled out her phone and miserably texted Sloane:

Can you go to the farmers' market and find Norma Cooke? Her great-aunt married Thomas Zimmerman. She might know something about his baby.

After a moment, Amelia added:

You might want to bring along some money for bribes.

Hopefully Slayer Sloane would have better luck than Amelia the Yeti.

9

Horrifying Discoveries at the Farmers' Market

Sloane stared incredulously at Amelia's text about bribes. However, she had to admit that the other girl frequently had good ideas even if they seemed kinda strange at first. With a shrug, Sloane emptied out her piggy bank. It actually had quite a lot in it, thanks to her recent birthday.

Had she only known it, Sloane was about to pay money to get someone *else* closer to the missing Hoäl treasure too.

Someone who had watched Amelia's YouTube video with interest. Someone who had just sent the girls a box of letters discovered in an old house at another estate sale three months before.

Someone who had excellent aim with a slingshot.

Had she known that, Sloane still would have paid the money.

(But Slayer Sloane would have brought along her own slingshot to the cemetery later in the week. Because it would have been game *on.*)

However, Sloane didn't know any of this. Right now, she thought the idea that anyone might be using them was just paranoia. Right now, Sloane had a much bigger problem in the form of Mac Attack Snyder and her blabby mouth. Which, unfortunately, could not be fixed with a slingshot.

Sloane's dad walked with her up to the farmers' market on North Fulton Street. She was surprised by how easy it had been to convince him. Not only had he worked all day, he'd ordered pizza for supper so he could work on putting new tile in one of the bathrooms. And he'd *hummed while doing it.* Now, rather than being too tired, he'd said, "That sounds great! I think I'll go too!" when Sloane mentioned where she was going.

When he said "great," her dad sounded like he really meant it too.

Sloane didn't know what to make of any of it.

However, she wasn't nicknamed "Slayer" for nothing. As they crossed the railroad tracks that separated South Fulton Street from North Fulton Street, she forced herself to focus on the task at hand. Amelia was counting on her, and she was not about to let a friend down. Not a real friend like Amelia, just because she was having trouble with a fake friend like Mackenzie.

About a dozen canvas tents lined the sidewalk on either side of the street in front of the old brick storefronts. They were divided pretty much evenly between people selling food and people selling crafts. The food included things like vegetables, goat cheese, cookies, bread, and honey. The crafts were things like fleece hats and homemade soaps, the second of which her dad stopped to check out.

"Hey, you don't know where Norma Cooke is, do you?" Sloane asked the beekeeper next to the soap stand.

"That lunatic?" This from a guy who regularly shoved his hand into hives housing thousands of bees so he could steal from them. "She's over that way."

Sloane followed his thumb toward a purple tent. It was the only tent that wasn't either white or emblazoned with Ohio State or University of Michigan decals. While her dad chatted with the cute soap maker, Sloane went over to the purple tent.

The front had been decorated with leftover Christmas tinsel, along with a string of lights. A swirly sign said GLAMOROUS GOOSE GARMENTS. Within the tent, there were racks and racks of small outfits.

All of them intended to be worn by concrete goose garden ornaments.

One of Sloane's neighbors, Mrs. Rice, had a concrete goose that she kept on her front porch. She dressed it in a yellow raincoat and hat for most of the year but changed it into a pumpkin costume at Halloween and a Santa costume at Christmas.

Sloane didn't get it at all.

However, Mrs. Rice's obsession with fashion for her garden decorations was nothing compared to Norma Cooke's. Several concrete geese modeled her creations throughout the tent. One wore a feather boa and sparkly evening gown. Another was dressed like Queen Elizabeth the first, while another was very clearly an homage to Lady Gaga.

Amelia would probably totally get this.

Sloane's mouth just hung open as she went, "Errrrrr . . ."

"Bonjour, my dear!" An elderly woman wearing a green satin turban on her head and a long purple dress swept forward to greet Sloane. "What has sparked your interest in unique lawn ornament fashions this fair, glorious twilight?"

Yup, Amelia would totally get her.

"Do you perhaps desire a bikini for your stone soul mate?" Norma held up a sequined swimsuit with matching sunglasses and floppy hat. "Or perhaps you wish to capture the joie de vivre of the 1920s with your very own flapper frock for your fake feathered friend?"

Sloane wasn't sure how much of that she actually understood. However, she was still positive that the answer was no.

"Uh, no. Um, you're Norma Cooke, right?" Sloane sort of hoped she wasn't.

"In the flesh!" the woman twinkled, booping Sloane on the nose with a gloved finger. She wore long green satin gloves that matched the turban on her head. "The *propriétaire d'entreprise* of Glamorous Goose Garments! How might I make your lawn ornaments more stylish? Perhaps they wish to be Marilyn Monroe in *The Seven Year Itch*?"

"Um, no. What I'd actually like—"

"Cher at the 1986 Oscar awards?"

"Wow—that's . . . sparkly. But—"

"Ah! I know! Now I have you pegged!" The woman had been swooshing various miniature outfits in front of Sloane's nose. Now she brought out something sternly black with lots of white lace. "Queen Victoria!"

"Yes! Yes! I'll take that!" Sloane grabbed the garment desperately and clung to it like it might give her the strength of an extremely stern-looking monarch. Then, all on its own, her mouth babbled, "Um, and the—er, Queen Elizabeth dress, too."

Where on earth had that come from? Sheer terror, that was where. Sloane had no idea how to deal with this woman.

"Do you want the wig as well?" Norma clasped her hands together in delight and peered out at Sloane over bejeweled spectacles.

"Sure, why not?" Sloane agreed wearily, sincerely wishing that Amelia was here to speak this woman's language. Her partner was counting on her, and Slayer Sloane had never—not once—let a teammate down.

Norma Cooke tucked the two goose-sized costumes into a purple-and-green bag while humming happily. Sticking her head outside the tent, Sloane saw that her dad was still chatting away with the soap lady. Whatever deal he was striking, Sloane hoped it was better than the one she was getting.

"Norma—Mrs. Cooke—may I call you Norma?" Sloane pulled out her wallet.

"You may call me a Beam of Moonlight Who Has Been Trapped on This Earth to Bedazzle It with Her Creativity," Norma announced grandly, punching at an old-fashioned-looking adding machine.

"Yeah, okay. So, Mrs. Moonbeam—my name is Sloane Osburn and I need to ask you a few questions about your great-aunt Beatrice." Sloane started to take her money out of her wallet and then thought better of handing it over. Trying to imagine herself as Amelia, she fanned her face with it. That seemed like the dramatic sort of thing the other girl would do.

Instead of perking up, Norma Moonbeam's face crumpled. A moment before, she'd been full of cheer. She yanked the lever on her adding machine and said, "Oh, *that* woman. Mother always said Great-Auntie Beatrice was very strict and stern. She died before I was born, but she and Cousin Ozzie lived with Mama and Grandma for years while Ozzie grew up. She'd always snap at Mama and Ozzie that children should be seen and not heard. I know it sounds terrible, but Mama said that the day Great-Auntie died was one of the happiest of her life."

Yikes. *How strict and stern did your aunt have to be for a funeral to rank up there with Christmas?* Sloane wondered as she handed over her money. "Can you tell me about her? And her kid?"

"Oh, well. Cousin Ozzie wasn't so bad." Norma perked up a bit, though that might have been from the money.

"Ozzie?"

"That's what we called Oscar. Who names their child Oscar? Even in 1887 people didn't do that." Norma counted the bills Sloane had given her. "Say, you're about five dollars short."

Another five dollars? Sloane had given her fifty; most of her birthday money. How much could it cost to dress something that sat out in the yard and got rained on? Reluctantly, Sloane peeled off a five and handed it to Norma.

That kept her talking, at least. "Of course, Ozzie was a grown-up by the time I was born—and quite a successful businessman at that! Very, very rich."

"What did he do?" Sloane asked. "I thought Beatrice didn't have any money."

"Oh . . . well . . ." That gave Norma pause. She set down the money she'd been counting and tapped her lip thoughtfully. "Do you know? I don't think that I know what Ozzie did. He didn't make his money until after Great-Auntie Beatrice passed away, from what Mama said. He'd always worked so hard, but things never seemed to go right for him until his mother died. Then all of a sudden, whatever his business was, it must have really taken off. Because he had enough money to share with the whole family!"

It sounded to Sloane very much like Cousin Ozzie hadn't suddenly become successful. More like he'd suddenly discovered the location of a whole bunch of stolen gems worth a great deal of money.

"Did he keep on living here in Wauseon?" Sloane asked as Norma finished tucking the goose costumes into the purple-and-green bag.

"No, he moved down to the Old West End in Toledo with the rest of the millionaires." Norma handed Sloane the bag by its handles. "Lovely doing business with you!"

"Did he ever get married and have kids? What was his address?" Sloane asked, tucking the bag under her arm so she could tap notes into her phone. Maybe Ozzie had taken after his dad and built hidden compartments too. And maybe some of the jewels were still there. "Did he ever talk about what had happened with—well, with . . . you know?"

Behind her bejeweled glasses, Norma blinked several times in confusion.

"The . . . robbery?" Sloane prompted.

"Oh, you must mean when Ozzie lost all of his money right before World War Two." Suddenly, all of Norma's fluttery, sparkly joy disappeared. "I don't think I want to talk about that."

So she didn't, abruptly turning her back on Sloane. She hummed as she brushed away imaginary specks of dust from a concrete goose modeling a pink-and-gold feathered headdress.

Meanwhile, the wheels in Sloane's brain spun out all sorts of ideas. Ozzie, Thomas's son, had been mysteriously rich only to suddenly lose it all. Was it possible that he'd kept the money in that secret compartment all that time? If so, had that note been left for him? Had someone robbed the robber's son?

Did that mean the baby they were looking for was Charles? He'd come back to Wauseon right before World War II as well!

"Um, Norma? I mean, Mrs. Moonbeam?" Sloane prodded, but the woman kept her back turned to Sloane and hummed louder. When Sloane tried to stand next to her, Norma immediately turned away to straighten the velvet hangers holding various little outfits.

Oh, for the love of . . . Sloane closed her eyes in exasperation. She'd already spent most of her birthday money; she might as well spend the last ten dollars, too.

Opening her eyes again, she looked around for something else to buy.

Hang on a moment—was that a *Doctor Who* costume? The Fourth Doctor, from the olden days? Sloane snatched up the brown overcoat, striped scarf, and brimmed hat. "I'd like to buy this too, please."

Turning around, Norma brightened up once more. "Lovely!"

"But maybe you could tell me about Ozzie losing his money while I pay?" Sloane suggested.

Tears glistened in Norma's eyes and her lips wobbled as she whispered theatrically, "It was a terribly difficult time. One day Ozzie had money, and the next it was just gone. I was at their house in the Old West End the day it happened. He'd been out here to Wauseon on business, and I was at home with his wife and son,

Johnny. We couldn't make sense of anything he was saying, and before we knew it, he'd rushed out of the house again. I don't know what he planned on doing, but he was in such a state that he—that he—well, he stepped right in front of a streetcar. And that was the end of dear Ozzie."

A tear trickled out of Norma's eye and plopped onto the adding machine. Sloane wished she had a tissue to offer her. Since she didn't, Norma took off one of her gloves and used it to wipe her eyes instead.

She continued, "It was then that we found out that there was no money in his bank account. Where he got his money from, none of us knew. Invested in the stock market, I assumed. But if he did, we couldn't find any evidence of it. Ozzie always said that Beatrice told him a secret when she was dying that helped make him rich. Maybe so, but whatever it was, the secret died with him. His wife and son lost everything. And then the little boy went bad when he grew up—ended up in prison, I heard."

"Did you say his name was Johnny Zimmerman?"

"Oh, no. It would be Johnny Kerr. Ozzie always went by Kerr, his mother's last name. Something about his father being a disgrace to the family and people around town treating Great-Auntie Beatrice like she had the plague for marrying him."

Having finished, Norma picked up a spare concrete goose and handed it to Sloane. Fortunately, Sloane had some good muscles from softball practice or she would have dropped it onto her foot. Even as it was, her arms sagged.

"Here, take one of my geese. That way yours can have a friend." Norma patted Sloane on the cheek.

Sloane didn't have the heart to tell her that she didn't actually have a concrete goose. She supposed that at least now she had something to put all of the costumes on. While hiding it deep at the back of her closet where no one would ever, ever see it.

Staggering under the weight of her new garden ornament, Sloane went to find her dad. However, it was much easier than she thought it would be as he was still at the soap booth, talking to the soap lady.

Who was really quite pretty, Sloane realized.

And about the same age as her dad.

As Sloane watched, he reached forward and plucked a bit of cottonwood fluff from her shoulder. Like this wasn't the first time they'd met.

Like he knew her well, in fact.

Uuuuuugggghhhhh. The concrete goose dragged Sloane slowly downward until she was sitting on the curb, her stomach all knotted up again.

Now he was laughing—*laughing*! Sloane hadn't heard him do that since her mom died. Not really. Not real laughter.

Sloane thought she might puke into the gutter.

"How's it going, Sloane-y?" Like a bad witch, Mackenzie seemed to materialize out of thin air. Somewhere in whatever demon dimension she'd come from, she'd found a doughnut to buy and munch on. "Got anything for me yet?"

Getting up slowly, Sloane narrowed her eyes and poked Mackenzie with the goose's beak. "How about a concrete goose dropped on your foot?"

"I'm not scared of you," Mackenzie sneered, and took another bite of her doughnut. "But I bet Amelia will be once she finds out *you* were the one who got everyone to call her 'Yeti' this past month."

"That's not how it happened. And besides, it's your word against mine, Mac."

"I thought you might say that." Grinning, the other girl pulled out her phone and tapped up a video. It was awkwardly filmed, and for some reason, Mackenzie had done so while using a filter that gave Sloane Easter Bunny ears and a cute little nose.

Even so, it was very definitely Sloane standing in the library.

A hurt, angry digital Sloane said, "She's like a yeti herself. A hairy, weird, dramatic yeti. Amelia the Yeti."

Real-life Sloane flinched and ground her teeth together, feeling more than ever like she might throw up. Waves of shame, regret, grief, and anger hit her one after the other until she thought they might drag her away completely.

And maybe they did. Certainly, Sloane didn't feel like herself as she stood there and whispered, "Thomas Zimmerman had a son, Oscar. I think he might have known what happened to the jewels."

Mackenzie smiled evilly and slowly took another bite of her doughnut. "See? That wasn't so hard. Did he tell anyone where they went?"

"I don't know."

"Well, it's not much. But it'll do. For now." The other girl tucked her phone back into her pocket and swaggered off.

The soap lady handed Sloane's dad a bag. When their hands touched, they held them there and looked into each other's eyes.

Sloane wished she had her mother here to hug.

Crazily, she wished she had Amelia here to talk to as well.

But she wasn't lucky enough to have anyone to talk to or hug.

All she had was this bizarre stone goose, cold and heavy in her hands.

10

SLOANE AND AMELIA REALIZE
SOMEONE IS WATCHING THEM

Sloane's dad helped her carry the concrete goose home.

"Wow. This is . . . not what I would have expected you to get at the farmers' market." He panted, struggling under its weight as they reached the front porch.

"Present for my grannies," Sloane managed to say. It seemed like the only logical thing to do with it.

"Now that makes a little more sense." Her dad set the goose down on their porch, and they both went in out of the blue twilight to the welcoming gold of the foyer. "What do you think about the soap I got?"

"I don't like the smell of lavender," Sloane said, and then fled upstairs. She knew it had been rude, but they were the only words her brain could come up with. She didn't like lavender and she didn't like the soap lady, either.

Her mom would have *hated* the soap lady.

Who did that woman think she was? Sloane wondered that night as she got around for bed. Scowling into the mirror, she brushed her teeth furiously. The soap lady hadn't looked even a little bit like she would enjoy watching old cheesy *Doctor Who* episodes. And she definitely looked like someone who would make a face at the thought of bacon-and-banana-pepper pizza.

Having washed her face and changed into her pajamas, Sloane looked longingly at her phone. She thought about trying to video-chat Amelia, but what if one of the other Miller-Poes overheard them? She could only imagine the advice they'd have to give, when it was Amelia's opinion Sloane wanted, not theirs.

In the end, Sloane spent a restless night, then scuttled off to school early the next morning. She found Amelia in Mr. Roth's English classroom. However, one snarky look from Mackenzie stopped all of the words about to come out of Sloane's mouth about her dad. No way was she going to say anything that might give her volleyball teammate more ammunition.

Besides, Amelia immediately wanted to talk about what they'd both found out. "Can you believe it?" The other girl gasped dramatically. "Who would have thought that after a hundred and thirty years, we—"

However, before she could finish, Sloane noticed Mackenzie sidling toward them under the pretense of sharpening her pencil. She shushed Amelia and in a loud voice said, "Yeah, I wished I'd found out more too. I mean, a hundred-and-thirty-year-old mystery, right? What can Mr. Roth possibly expect us to find?"

Squinting at them suspiciously, Mackenzie used the sharpener and sat back down.

In Amelia's ear, Sloane hissed, "Not here. Want to meet at the library after softball practice?"

Amelia nodded her head vigorously. "It'll be a secret meeting!

Like there are spies watching us who have nefarious plans to steal our valuable clues!"

For once, Amelia wasn't exaggerating even if she didn't know it. That was *exactly* what this was like.

Though, to be fair, Sloane was also unaware of just how many people were watching them.

After school, Sloane went to softball practice and then stopped by her dad's orthodontist office for a snack since it was on the way to the library. However, when Sloane got to the building, she didn't find him with his hands in some poor kid's mouth. Instead, her dad was in his office.

And the soap lady was there with him.

Today she was wearing a suit and had a number of pamphlets and sample retainers she was showing him.

At first, Sloane thought, *Whew! He just knows her from work. That's all.*

Then she noticed that the soap lady was sitting on his desk.

And the two of them were laughing again. Together.

"Sloane!" Her dad spotted her and stood up abruptly. The woman on his desk quickly became the woman standing next to his desk, an awkward (and slightly terrified) smile plastered across her face as he continued, "This is—this is—"

"The soap lady," Sloane finished for him.

"Oh, that's just my hobby." The soap lady's smile was more awkward and terrified than ever. So much so that Sloane glanced over her shoulder to confirm that there wasn't some sort of ginormous, hairy monster standing behind her. Nope, just

Sloane. The soap lady continued, "My name is Cynthia Seife. It's lovely to meet you, Sloane. I knew your mother professionally, and she was a wonderful woman."

Wow. Cynthia Seife might as well have picked up one of the tooth scrapers and jammed it right into Sloane's heart. In fact, it felt very much like she had.

"Yeah, my dad thought she was pretty great too."

Her dad and Cynthia Seife exchanged a look. No—wait. They didn't exchange it, they *shared* it. Like he and her mom used to do!

"I'd better be going." Cynthia "The Soap Lady" Seife swept all her orthodontic gear into her briefcase and skedaddled out of the office. She squeezed past Sloane like she thought Sloane might bite.

A terrible realization occurred to Sloane. One that had nothing to do with either treasure or people who might be using her to find it. "Wait a second! *She's* why you're going to that dumb orthodontics dinner over in Archbold on Saturday rather than staying in and watching *Doctor Who* with me!"

"I thought you didn't mind if I went!"

"That's before I knew you were dumping me for someone else! Mom would never have done that to me!" Her dad's eyes went wide with pain, but Sloane didn't care. She was glad she'd hurt him. He totally deserved it, betraying Sloane like that. Betraying her mom like that! Sloane snatched up her backpack again. "Forget it! I've got to go. I'm meeting Amelia at the library."

"Sloane, wait!" her dad called after her, but she ignored him. Instead, Sloane practically ran the distance from his office to the library.

What if her dad married this Cynthia Seife? What if he had a new family with her?

What if they moved houses? What if her dad was only fixing up their house so he could sell it?

That was the house where Sloane used to ride her tricycle in the attic in the winter while her mom chased her, pretending to be a monster. All because Sloane had once been scared that there might be monsters up there. Her mom had done it so that when Sloane thought of the monsters, she'd also think about laughing and having fun together.

What if she had to move into a new house where there were just monsters in the attic and no memories of laughter?

Sloane already felt like she wasn't really living her own life at school. What if she lost her life at home too?

She pushed open the glass library doors and trudged up the steps. She found Amelia waiting for her at one of the research tables. The other girl was wearing a trench coat and brimmed hat over the black turtleneck and leggings she'd worn when breaking into the historical society the other day. Sloane assumed that this was the other girl's take on what a spy would wear to a secret meeting.

A box filled with old letters sat on the table in front of her.

"What's got you so upset?" Amelia asked as Sloane sat down.

Sloane's eyes almost bugged out of her head. "What makes you think I'm upset about something? I'm not upset about something."

"Well, you're playing with your ponytail, and you only ever do that when you're upset or nervous," Amelia pointed out.

Sloane realized that she was, in fact, playing with her ponytail.

None of her other friends had ever picked up on that before. If Mackenzie ever had, she would have already found a way to use that knowledge for evil.

Everything finally came tumbling out, as if Sloane had stuffed so much back down into her soul that there wasn't room for anything else.

Amelia listened solemnly, and when Sloane was done, the other girl clasped her hands together, eyes misty with emotion. "You feel it is an insult to the memory of your beloved mother for your dad to date. He should spend his nights weeping by her photograph, bringing flowers to her grave, and casting himself upon her tombstone—"

"No, no, no! Nothing like that. Jeez." Sloane gnawed at some tendrils of hair. "It's just that I think Granny Kitty is right about him figuring out how to live his life again. But I'm not sure I'm figuring out how to live mine, and—and—Amelia, I'm really sorry about being mean to you. Before, I mean. Like, not just when we started this project. But even before it."

"Oh. Well." Amelia blinked rapidly. "That's okay. You weren't ever really mean to me."

"No, it isn't okay, and I was. And I'm sorry." It was on the tip of Sloane's tongue to confess everything. To tell Amelia that it was her fault that everyone had been calling her "Yeti" this past month. But she just couldn't—quite—go that far.

Because they were definitely becoming friends—and that would stop the second Amelia knew the truth.

Sloane would be left with nothing but fake friends like

Mackenzie, who only liked her because she could spike the ball.

Thinking the crisis had passed, Amelia glanced around. Making sure there weren't any other seventh graders in the library—just Milton doing a Harry Potter sock puppet show for some elementary kids over in the corner—she shoved a book in Sloane's direction before burying her nose in a book of her own.

"Just casually read your book," Amelia whispered. "In case anyone is watching."

Like who? Bunny? Milton's sock puppets?

Sloane opened her book and pretended to read.

"*Ssssmmmunn ssnntt muh tha baahxxx uh ledderrrss,*" Amelia mumbled through pressed lips.

"Excuse me?" Sloane said it too loudly, and apparently Bunny *had* been listening. He came over with his tail wagging and his tongue hanging out. She scratched his ears.

"Shh!" Amelia looked around furtively and then muttered again, "*Ssssmmmunn ssnntt muh tha baahxxx uh ledderrrss!*"

"Okay, I really have no idea what you're saying!" Sloane hissed.

Amelia scooted farther down in her chair and drew her hat to the tip of her nose. She still whispered, but at least she moved her lips this time. "Someone sent me that box of letters. It might be someone from school and it might be someone who watched the video I posted on YouTube. Right now, I'm guessing maybe Mr. Roth or Principal Stuckey. *But it's got to be someone who wants us to find the jewels.*"

Still pretending to read her book, Sloane casually hooked

the box with one finger and tugged it into her lap. Bunny peered at them with interest.

"These are from Jacob to Thomas. And Thomas to Jacob!" Sloane gasped.

"Shhhh!" Amelia warned again. "Some of them are. And then *others are from Charles to Oscar.*"

"What? They knew each other? No way!" Sloane thumbed through them and saw that Amelia was right. Meanwhile, Bunny realized they weren't treats and looked disappointed. "Okay, so Charles and Oscar knew each other somehow. We also know that Oscar lived somewhere in Toledo's Old West End and was mysteriously rich until one day he mysteriously wasn't. *And* we know that Charles went and lived with his grandparents in Toledo for a while, but by the late 1930s he was back in Wauseon."

"He was back in this area, but we don't know that he ever lived in Wauseon. Maybe instead he was living in the Hotel Waldorf!" Still pretending to read her book, Amelia pulled out the postcard Sloane had found and slid it across the table. "That was a thing a lot of people used to do, you know. Live in hotels."

"It was not."

"It was so."

"She's right." Belinda came over to get Bunny. She had a specially designed halter with pouches on either side that allowed him to carry books that she needed to shelve.

She seemed extremely well informed about local history. Granted, she *was* a librarian, but still.

And she always seemed to be mysteriously around, listening.

Belinda sat down next to them. "If you want, I can show you

how to look up census records, since you can't just search for them online. You have to have a subscription, which the library does."

Hmm. Sloane and Amelia exchanged a look. Had the librarian sent them the box of letters? If so, she was hiding it well now. Reluctantly, they agreed, and handed her Amelia's Chromebook.

"The census keeps track of where every person in the country lives once every ten years," Belinda explained as she tapped at the keyboard. "When do you want to look?"

That was a good question. Sloane pulled out the postcard of the Hotel Waldorf. "You don't have any idea when this dates to, do you?"

"Haven't a clue. That's Milton's area of expertise, not mine." They all looked over at the museum curator. He was so into his reenactment of the end of *The Chamber of Secrets* that several first graders were clinging to each other and scooting backward as a snake sock puppet dived repeatedly at the Harry Potter sock puppet.

"I don't think now's a good time to ask him," Amelia observed.

Belinda shrugged and pulled up the database. "So, what are we looking for?"

"Why don't we look for Oscar Kerr first?" Sloane shuffled through her notes. "Try 1920, 1930, 1940, and 1950."

Belinda did as she asked. "Looks like he and his mom were still living in Wauseon in 1920. However, by 1930, his mom was dead and Oscar was married to someone named Shirley. He must have been doing really well for himself because they lived in the Old West End, which was pretty fancy back then. Um, in 1940, they were still living there and had a one-year-old son named Johnny.

And then—uh-oh. By 1950, things had gotten a *lot* worse for everyone. Oscar was dead, and Shirley and Johnny Kerr were living in a pretty shabby part of town."

"Can you see what year Oscar died?" Amelia leaned over Belinda's shoulder. Bunny put his paws up on the table and tried to figure out what was so fascinating about the computer.

Belinda switched to a different database. This one had birth, marriage, and death records. "Wow. Not long after the census was taken in 1940, actually. Looks like he died on October eighth, 1940. Dude, that's sad. His dad died before he could see Oscar grow up, and then Oscar died before he could see *his* son grow up."

Sloane's throat closed tight at that, but she pushed back at the wave of sadness it made her feel. "Can you see who was staying at the Hotel Waldorf in 1940?"

"Not if they just stayed there for a night or two. But back then, lots of people would move into a hotel and stay there for months or even years. That way, someone else could do all of the cooking and cleaning." Belinda went back to the census's page, printed off the list of occupants for 1940, and gave it to them. "If you need anything else, let me know."

With that, she and Bunny walked off to shelve books. It didn't take very long for Sloane to find what they were looking for.

"A-HA!" Sloane jabbed her finger at the page. "Amelia—"

"Wait!" The other girl held up her phone so she could record. "Go!"

It was a little unnerving to know she was being filmed.

•

Sloane hoped she didn't look too weird. "You were right! In 1940, Charles Forrester Hoäl was living at the Hotel Waldorf!"

Amelia was so excited that she dropped the phone. With a squeak, she picked it up, almost dropped it again, and then managed to get a good grip on it.

Trying to sound as intelligent as she could for the camera, Sloane said, "What if Thomas managed to get a message to Beatrice back in 1887, telling her where he'd hidden the jewels? What if she wouldn't touch them because they were stolen and she didn't think it would be right, no matter how little money she had? What if she didn't tell anyone because she wanted to try to pretend Thomas was innocent? What if she told Oscar about it all on her deathbed? What if Charles Hoäl figured out where Oscar was getting his money—and stole back the jewels? *What if there's evidence of that in these letters?*"

"Hey, you're pretty good at being dramatic." Satisfied with what she'd filmed, Amelia switched the camera off. Her phone immediately dinged, causing Amelia to groan, "I've got to go. It's Miller-Poe Swim Night. That means we spend an hour doing laps."

To reinforce how awful it was, she pulled out a swim cap and tugged it on over her bushy red curls.

It made her look like a balding clown.

"At least they can't lecture you on your stroke if they're swimming too," Sloane pointed out.

"HA!" Amelia made a face. "The rest of my family has such amazing breath control that they can lecture me while swimming.

The lifeguards always seem pretty impressed. We'll divide up the letters and read them tonight?"

"Sure. I'll text you if I find anything especially interesting."

"Keep an eye out for anyone watching you." Amelia nodded toward Principal Stuckey, who was back in the cookbook section again.

Seeming to sense Amelia's and Sloane's eyes on her, their principal looked up. She smiled and nodded and then went back to reading cookie recipes. Was she really not interested in what they were doing—or was she a good actress?

"Mr. Roth is over there." Sloane jerked her head toward their teacher as he joined the elementary kids watching Milton's puppet show. He didn't even glance their way.

But perhaps he was too smart to let them know that he'd followed them there.

Was it coincidence that both Mr. Roth and Principal Stuckey were there?

Or were one or both of them using Sloane and Amelia to find the jewels?

Amelia shuffled off to meet her watery doom, leaving Sloane behind to worry about this. If she and Amelia *did* find the jewels, she didn't want someone else to swoop in and take them away. Especially since that person might do something horrible to the two of them in the process.

"What's up, Sloane-y Woney?" Mackenzie slid into Amelia's vacant chair, startling Sloane so badly that she actually yelped. That was the second time the other girl had managed to materialize out of thin air. Maybe she really was an evil witch. "Got anything for me? That bit about Thomas having a son named Oscar was barely enough for half a slide. I need more than that if I'm going to get an A on this project."

Sloane gaped at Mackenzie, grateful that she still had the letters hidden in her lap. Did she really think that Sloane was going to do all of her research for her?

Apparently so. Mackenzie reached for the stack of printouts. Feeling the heat rush to her face, Sloane snatched them up before the other girl could. She shoved everything into her backpack before Mac could spot the letters too.

"Forget it. You've gotten all you're going to get out of me." Sloane stood up, pretty sure her eyes were shooting daggers. Just not real ones, unfortunately.

"I was hoping you'd say that. Now I get to break Amelia's little heart. Anyone can see she thinks you're her friend. I can't wait to see her face when she finds out how wrong she is." Mackenzie stood up too.

Straightening the bow in her hair, she sashayed off.

Sloane's fingers itched to reach for her phone so she could text Mackenzie and beg her to reconsider, but she refused to let them do it. She had no idea what Mac had planned, but she was positive that the other girl would do it eventually no matter what Sloane did to try to please her.

Privately, she hoped that maybe she'd get lucky and whoever was trying to use them to find the jewels would think Mackenzie found them. Maybe they'd package Mac up and mail her off to Antarctica.

Somehow Sloane doubted it, and she was quite right about this.

When she and Amelia were attacked later that week, Mackenzie Snyder already would be grounded by her parents.

Which was very unlucky for the former Tootie Snyder.

And even less lucky for Sloane and Amelia.

11

Amanda Poe Has a Horrible Shock

Miller-Poe Swim Night was consistently horrific, and this Tuesday was no exception. Swim night managed to be worse than Friday golf night and Monday tennis night combined. At least Amelia was just bad at those other two sports. With swimming, the chlorine made her eyes burn, her skin itch, and her hair frizz.

Plus, she was at least somewhat less likely to drown while playing golf and tennis. Even if there were water hazards on the golf course and a creek by the tennis courts.

And she'd accidentally fallen into both. More than once.

Eager to get rid of the smells of chlorine and humiliation, Amelia took a shower in her big, sparkling white bathroom as soon as they got home. Then she retreated to her big, sparkling white bedroom to sit at a table that was also depressingly big, sparkling, and white. She'd put on a button-down shirt, one of her dad's ties, and a brimmed hat because that's what Humphrey Bogart had worn as the private investigator in the black-and-white movie *The Maltese Falcon*. Amelia had watched that one with her grandma Suzy the last time she was over at her grandma's house.

She got out her stack of the old letters. Before she looked at them, though, she pulled up her YouTube channel on her Chromebook to see how her video was doing. It had thirty likes and she'd gained ten more followers.

Amelia wondered if one of them was Mr. Roth or Principal Stuckey. She wasn't entirely sure that she *really* believed either one of them could be using her and Sloane.

But she wasn't sure she didn't believe it, either.

Certainly, *someone* had sent her these letters. Maybe they'd just done it to be nice.

Maybe.

Or maybe not. Belinda was a bit of a worry too, as was Mr. Neikirk. True, he didn't seem to know a lot about technology—but she bet his grandkids did. And he *definitely* knew a lot about old stuff. Maybe even more than he was telling them.

The lens of the Chromebook's camera stared back at her like an eye—or a spy hole. For the first time, a creepy-crawly feeling shivered its way across the back of her neck. She checked to make sure that her Chromebook's camera was turned off. Then, still not feeling entirely reassured, Amelia went ahead and shut it completely.

Her stack of letters was mostly from Charles to Oscar. However, the first letter was made of different paper than the others. It was thinner, more yellowed, and far shorter. Amelia's heart beat faster as she read it, for it cleared up one mystery right away. Thomas had quickly scrawled out a letter to his wife before he got onto that unlucky train.

My dearest Beatrice,

Please forgive me, for I've done something terrible, though I did it for you and Oscar. By now you'll know that the jewels are gone from the Hoäl mansion and that I took them. They are hidden inside a compartment on the other side of the fireplace from the safe, a secret that only I know about. However, I can no longer get to them without arousing suspicion. I have gone to Chicago to beg Jacob's forgiveness. If he does not give it to me, I will be imprisoned for many years, leaving you penniless. If you don't hear from me by tomorrow morning, he hasn't forgiven me and you must find some way to the jewels right away. Flee Wauseon and start a new life somewhere else, even if it means leaving behind your family. I know that you will think it is wrong and not want to do it. But how else will you take care of our son?

Your loving husband,
Thomas

Well, that sounded like a truly terrible plan to Amelia. Even without factoring in the bad luck of the train accident, there was no way this was ever going to work out well for Thomas. A criminal mastermind he most definitely was not.

Maybe the reason the plan was so bad was because he

wasn't naturally a bad person. Just one desperate to take care of his family.

The rest of the letters were all on a thicker paper that wasn't as yellowed as Thomas's. These were the ones that Charles had written to Oscar more than fifty years after Thomas had robbed Jacob.

October 8, 1940

Dear Oscar,

Do you remember the first time we met? We were both fifteen when the circus came to Toledo, where I lived with my grand-parents. You didn't know who I was, but I knew you as soon as I saw you pounding the tent pegs into the ground. You looked exactly like your father. I knew because my grandparents kept a copy of his picture so I would never forget what the monster looked like.

I expected you to be a monster too, and I planned on getting my father's revenge against your family. That was really why I joined the circus. Not to escape my grandparents, the way I told you. I didn't know how, but I was going to make your life miserable.

Instead, we ended up friends. Can you believe the luck? I should have hated you, but no matter how hard I tried, I could not. And so, I forgot my plans to make you suffer.

The circus life wasn't for me any more than it had been for my father. When I left it a few years later, I thought that you were happily living the life your father had always dreamed about.

How wrong I was.
Charles

Huh. Oscar and Charles had been friends just like their fathers. Who would have thought it? Although, it sounded like only Charles had actually known about their dads at the time. They'd both joined the circus too, and eventually fallen out and become enemies. Amelia couldn't decide if that was bad luck or bad choices.

Either way, Mr. Roth was going to be so totally impressed with what she and Sloane had discovered—whether or not he was using them to find the location of the jewelry.

The next letter was dated only two days later on October 10, 1940.

Imagine my surprise when I discovered that you were no longer with the traveling circus! Not only that, you had grown quite rich. I lost all my money in the stock market crash of 1929. Yet you were rich. And your answers about how you had come by your money made no sense.

There was more to the letter after that, but it was mostly Charles venting angrily about the mystery of Oscar's money. He was understandably angry that he didn't have any money because Oscar's dad, Thomas, had taken it and Oscar himself had spent it.

Honestly, Amelia thought it was pretty stinky of Oscar not to give Charles back Jacob and Lucretia's jewels. Especially now that he knew that Charles had lost all of his money.

This was reinforced by a letter the next day that included this:

Why? Why wouldn't you give me the money I needed to pay Dr. Hadley to save my darling Lucy's life? Why did you let her die? You have a son, though he is still a baby. Do you think I loved my Lucy any less because she was an adult with a baby of her own? I would have done anything to save her. The treatment to cure her cancer could have worked. Why would you not give me the money I needed? It was rightfully my money, not yours. Yet you cruelly kept it from me.

Tears welled up in Amelia's eyes as she read Charles's words. What a horrible person Oscar must have been! Just like his equally terrible father. What sort of person stole money from a person trying to save his daughter's life?

She couldn't help but feel glad that Charles had managed to steal the jewels back from Oscar. They were his, so he should be able to do whatever he wanted with them. Maybe Oscar hadn't believed he was hurting anyone to keep the jewels when he thought that Oscar was still rich too. However, once he knew that his former friend wasn't—and that the jewels were Charles's anyway—what sort of monster wouldn't give them back? Especially when Charles needed to get his daughter those cancer treatments?

The injustice of it really burned Amelia up inside. Forget what she used to think about Thomas not being a bad person. She bet he was every bit as lazy and dishonest as those old newspapers had painted him to be. And his son was even worse.

The last letter was from October 12, 1940.

You thought I wouldn't figure out your secret, didn't you? You thought the jewels were safe inside the secret panel in my father's mansion. Did your mother really leave them there for all those years afterward? I bet she thought the jewels were cursed.

Ha! Amelia had been right. They *were* the Cursed Hoäl Jewels.

Not really the point, of course. But it always felt good to be proven right.

You left the jewels in the house, thinking them safe where no one had found them for all these years. In the mansion you thought I had left to rot. You didn't know I would return and try to turn the building into apartments. I did it after you refused to give me any money. That way, I could rent out the apartments to try to raise money for my beloved Lucy. Imagine my shock when I found the secret compartment! Now I know your little secret. Did you like the surprise I left for you in there? You made me suffer, so now I will make you suffer. Solve the riddle and the jewels will once more be yours. If you can't—then you can go back to being a clown. That's what you really are. Just someone who makes people laugh.

Except Oscar Kerr hadn't suffered. He'd died right after he got this letter. Actually, from what Norma Cooke said, maybe he never even read this letter. He discovered the jewels were gone and then stumbled in front of that streetcar. Probably before he even thought about checking the mail.

Then Charles had died not long afterward, and it all seemed terribly unfair to Amelia. Oscar *should* have suffered for letting this Lucy person die. Charles certainly did.

It was all very sad, but Amelia didn't see how this got them any closer to figuring out where the jewels were now hidden. Maybe whoever had sent the letters really was just a fan.

"Find the baby, find the jewels," but what baby? It couldn't be either Charles or Oscar, so what baby could it be? Charles's letter mentioned that his daughter Lucy had a baby, so Amelia supposed they'd have to find her now. Although . . . wait. The baby could be Oscar's son, though that seemed unlikely. What was his name again? Johnny? Johnny Kerr?

Up until now, none of the clues Amelia and Sloane had discovered about the missing Hoäl jewels had been caused by either serendipity or zemblanity. Every last bit of information they had uncovered had been due to one of two causes: either the unseen hand of the person who was using the seventh grade, or the hard work of Amelia and Sloane themselves.

What happened next was due entirely to serendipity.

(Or zemblanity, depending on how you looked at it. In just a few moments, Amelia would have definitely blamed zemblanity, if she only knew the word.)

"Amelia? What on earth are you doing?" Her mom stumbled

sleepily into the room, rubbing her hair so that it stood up like she'd been electrocuted. She wore black-and-white silk pajamas that looked exactly like the suits she wore during the day.

"I'm working on my project for English, Mom."

"Well! I'm very proud to see you applying yourself so diligently to your schoolwork!" Her mom beamed. "Though you should have Aiden or Ashley look it over before you turn it in."

"Sure, Mom." Amelia reached for one of the notes she'd stuck to the wall, knowing what was coming next.

"Here, let me help you clean up."

"Sure, Mom," Amelia agreed listlessly. Time to return her room to the way her mom wanted it to look. That right-out-of-a-designer-magazine perfectness that made it feel like it wasn't really her room at all.

Amanda Poe, however, froze as she picked up her first Post-it. In a strangled voice, quite unlike her usual bark, she said, "Amelia?"

"Yes, Mom?"

"Why do you—how do you—why does this note have your grandfather's name on it?" her mom finally managed.

Amelia just blinked at her in confusion. She knew it was late and that she was tired, but that didn't make a bit of sense.

"Huh?" Amelia said.

"Why are you researching your grandfather?" her mom demanded, waving the piece of paper about like it was evidence of a crime. "How did you find out his name? Have you been talking to Grandma Suzy? I told her that I didn't want her talking to you about him!"

Amelia tried blinking several more times. Maybe she'd fallen asleep and was dreaming. "Mom, who are you talking about? Do you mean Oscar Kerr? He's the son of Thomas Zimmerman, who stole a fortune in jewels over a hundred years ago."

"Oh, don't be ridiculous," her mom scoffed. "I mean Johnny Kerr, of course. John Kerr. My father. Though I don't think he can correctly be called that given that he tried to rob a bank and ended up in prison pretty much right after I was born."

Amelia knew most of that already because Grandma Suzy had told Amelia even though she wasn't supposed to. She also knew that Grandpa John had gotten sick in prison and died there. However, Grandma Suzy had just called him "John," and Amelia always thought of her real grandpa as Grandpa Lloyd Poe, who'd married Grandma Suzy when Amelia's mom was five. He'd adopted Amanda and helped raise her.

Amelia had never really bothered to think about the father her mom had started out with. Lloyd was nice and John had abandoned her mom and grandma. What else was there to know?

A great deal, as it turned out.

"Mom, Johnny Kerr was the son of Oscar Kerr, who was the son of Thomas Zimmerman, Fulton County's most notorious robber. Well, until everyone forgot about him and he stopped being notorious," Amelia explained. Her mom continued to stare at her like Amelia was babbling nonsense. "That means you're the great-granddaughter and I'm the great-great-granddaughter of a notorious robber. Who, uh, also accidentally caused the events that made two trains crash into each other, killing a whole bunch of people."

Other kids had always treated Amelia like she was a freak. Like she was defective somehow. For all the teasing, for all the times they had made her cry, Amelia had always told herself that they were wrong.

Now she wasn't so sure.

Her great-great-grandfather, great-grandfather, and grand-father were all thieves.

What if being defective was in her blood?

12

THINGS KEEP GETTING WORSE FOR AMELIA & SLOANE

While Amelia's recent discovery was due to either serendipity (if you consider that she'd just discovered another important clue) or zemblanity (if you consider that the clue in question involved the fact that she came from a long line of criminals), Sloane was currently dealing with a problem that had nothing to do with luck, either good or bad.

As with many problems in life, her current troubles were all deliberately caused by other people, as well as herself. If only she'd fessed up to starting the whole business, Mackenzie wouldn't have been able to intimidate her. If only Mackenzie were a nicer person and didn't feel threatened by Amelia's sudden rise in the world, she wouldn't be trying to bring her down again.

However, Sloane hadn't fessed up and Mackenzie wasn't a nice person. Luck couldn't be blamed for either of those things.

Earlier that evening and across town from Amelia, Sloane had slinked off for home after leaving the library. Her feet had moved slowly, without their usual energy. Bleakly, she supposed that at least there was a good side to Mackenzie's threats: they kept her mind off of her dad and the soap lady. Whatever was going on with them was probably a bigger problem than Mac, but it *was* a less immediate one. She needed to figure out what to do about Mackenzie right away. That bought her a little time before she had to figure out what to do about her dad.

At least Sloane knew what she had to do to beat Mackenzie at her own game.

Confess.

The trouble of it was, she didn't know *how* to confess without leaving Amelia feeling betrayed. Probably, she should do it as dramatically as possible. She should throw herself at Amelia's feet, crying. No, weeping. Sloane wasn't entirely certain what the difference was, but she was positive that Amelia would insist on weeping rather than crying. And would know if you tried to substitute one for the other.

That might very well work, but Sloane knew there was no way she could pull it off. She'd never been much of a crier, and while she felt bad that she'd accidentally started the whole "Yeti" business, she also didn't feel that meant she needed to throw herself at anyone's feet and beg forgiveness. Saying she was sorry was one thing. Begging was an entirely different matter.

It occurred to Sloane that she could get everyone to forget about Amelia the Yeti if she spread the news about Tootie Mackenzie the Farting Queen. If anyone deserved to be made fun of, it was definitely Mac.

However, Sloane found it very hard to believe that you made the world a better place for some people by making it even worse for others. Getting called names wouldn't make Mac any nicer or kinder; it would just make her meaner and then she'd take out all of that meanness on someone else.

Which pretty much left Sloane with confessing.

Both Granny Pearl and Granny Kitty were in the kitchen making goulash when Sloane came into the house through the kitchen door. A pot of noodles bubbled away on the old-fashioned stove's back burner, while Granny Pearl stirred a saucepan filled with beef and onions. Granny Kitty stood nearby, making a salad on the glossy new butcher-block counters.

"Sloane-y!" Much cheek-pinching and kissing followed.

When Sloane finally managed to free her face, her Amelia Problem suddenly seemed less important than her Dad Problem. Or maybe thinking about her Amelia Problem for a while had made it a bit easier to wrap her mind around her Dad Problem. "Um, Grannies? Did you guys know about Cynthia Soapy? I mean, Cynthia Seife?"

Granny Pearl and Granny Kitty exchanged a look.

"I'll get the ice cream," Granny Pearl said.

"I'll get the potato chips," Granny Kitty said.

Before Sloane knew it, she was shoved into a chair at the table and handed a pint of praline pecan and a bag of salt-and-pepper chips. Her grannies set down across from her and said simultaneously, "Yes."

"Oh, great! I'm the only one who *didn't* know." Sloane pushed the pint of ice cream away in a fit of anger. Then she thought better of it, grabbed it back, peeled off the lid, and tucked into it.

"She's very nice," Granny Kitty said hesitantly. "Your mom would have liked her."

"And neither your dad nor Cynthia wanted you to know they were dating until they were sure that they were going to be together for the long term," Granny Pearl added gently.

"'Long term'? Like, getting married?" Sloane gasped from around a mouthful of sugared pecans and caramel.

"They're not to that point yet!" Granny Pearl patted Sloane's hand. "That's why David hadn't introduced you to her But . . . maybe someday. Or maybe they'll date for a few months and then break up. But no matter what, Sloane, your dad loves you. We all do."

There was that, Sloane supposed, feeling a bit better.

Not a lot. But a bit.

Since her dad had to work late, her grannies stayed and had supper with Sloane, trading the junk food for the goulash. She helped them clean up the dishes and then went up to her room to read the letters that Amelia had given her, more than happy to lose herself in someone else's problems for a while.

December 4, 1886

Dear Thomas,

I am sorry to hear that Hoäl and Zimmerman Circus has gone out of business. I did warn you when I sold you my share of the circus that it was not making money. That your insistence on paying me twice what my share was worth was your fault, not mine. Yes, the money you gave me did help me to start my own business and win the hand of my darling wife, Lucretia.

However, I do not remember you saying that the extra money was an investment in my business. I am quite sure you said that it was a gift. Unless you have that deal in writing, I do not owe you anything.

In spite of these slanderous accusations against me, I am pleased to hear that you have recently married and now have a child on the way. I will not provide you with the money that you're asking for. However, in honor of our friendship and your excellent wood-carving skills, I will be more than happy to give you a job doing the woodwork on my new house. I'm afraid, however, that you will have to start at the lowest pay. Otherwise, it wouldn't be fair to the men who worked for years while you traveled with the circus.

Sincerely,
Jacob Hoäl

"Ugh. What a jerk," Sloane said to the concrete goose sitting in the corner of her room wearing the *Doctor Who* outfit. She made a face and tossed down the letter. From the sound of it, Thomas had loaned Jacob the money Jacob had used to become a millionaire. Then, when Thomas's business went bankrupt, Jacob never bothered to pay back his old friend.

No wonder Thomas had decided to rob Jacob! He must have felt that he was just taking back what was rightfully his.

It wasn't bad luck that had killed Thomas and Jacob and all of those other people on those two trains. They died because

Jacob had been greedy. If he'd been willing to share his wealth with the man who had helped him become rich, Thomas would never have become desperate. Then he never would have come up with that plan to blow up the safe and steal the jewels. Then all of the messages about the theft wouldn't have been getting telegraphed all over the place. The people running the railroad switches wouldn't have been distracted and those trains wouldn't have ended up on the same tracks.

Everyone would have lived.

There were other letters in here too, but they mostly seemed to be to Thomas from his wife, Beatrice, when he was still traveling with the circus and didn't have anything to do with the missing jewels. Sloane hoped Amelia's stack of letters had provided better clues about the location of the baby they were supposed to find.

The last letter in Sloane's stack wasn't from either Jacob or Beatrice, however. It wasn't even to Thomas. Instead, it was addressed to Oscar Kerr and was from some private investigator.

May 11, 1940

Dear Mr. Kerr,

As you suspected, the cure for cancer your friend is being offered is a scam. The tonic he swears will make the disease go away is actually nothing more than a little bit of arsenic in water. As arsenic is poisonous, it is more likely to kill the girl than to cure her. We would recommend not giving your friend the money for which he is asking. This doctor does nothing but take advantage of desperate people. Your friend's money would soon be gone and his daughter dead sooner rather than later.

Regards,
Spade Investigations

Sloane wondered what that was all about. She knew that arsenic was a type of poison, and telling people to drink it to "cure" them seemed like a very sick joke. She was glad that Oscar had been smart enough not to lend his friend the money, though she felt really bad for whoever it was that had the dying kid.

Still, Sloane couldn't imagine it had anything to do with the case.

Downstairs, the front door opened and keys jangled as they hit the tray that her dad kept them in. Sloane winced and her fingers reached for her hair.

However, she stopped them before they could touch her ponytail. Tugging on it wasn't going to solve anything. Honestly, Sloane didn't know what would.

But avoiding her problems wasn't going to solve them, either.

Slayer Sloane looked at the concrete goose in its *Doctor Who* clothes and told it, "I can do this."

Then she went downstairs.

Her dad was in the kitchen, warming up a plate of goulash that her grannies had left for him. When Sloane came in, he gave her a hesitant smile.

"Hey," he said.

"Hey," she said back.

Then neither one of them seemed to know what to say. At least they didn't say how great everything was.

"I'm sorry I ran out of your office earlier." It wasn't easy for Sloane to get the words out. Part of her brain seemed to think that if she kept them in, if neither one of them spoke about what happened, it would be like it hadn't really happened.

"I'm sorry I didn't tell you about Cynthia." Her dad looked down at the plate he was holding in his hands.

"Are you going to marry her?" Sloane blurted out.

"What?" Her dad was so surprised that he let go of the plate. He tried to catch it and almost did.

Almost, but not quite.

It crashed to the floor and cracked apart. Goulash splattered everywhere.

Sloane and her dad looked at it. Finally, he sighed. "Great. Just great."

"But it isn't great," Sloane said.

"I know." Bending down, he started picking up the broken pieces of plate. "And I don't know how to make it better."

Sloane knelt down next to him and helped. They tossed the broken pottery into the trash, and then she admitted. "Me neither. But I'm okay if things aren't always great. They don't always have to be."

When Sloane finished speaking, David Osburn did something he hadn't allowed himself to do in a long time.

He allowed himself to look sad.

The last time he'd looked like that—*really* looked like that—it had been Sloane's mom's funeral. Ever since then, Sloane realized, both of them had been determined to be strong for each other. To prove that as long as they had each other, it was enough.

Except it wasn't.

Sloane needed friends like Amelia. Real friends, not fake friends like Mackenzie.

And her dad needed someone to love him. Maybe someone like Cynthia Seife. Maybe someone else.

Either way, Sloane's grannies were right: they'd all still love each other.

Having cleaned up the mess, Sloane sat with her dad while he ate his goulash. Afterward, she went back up to her room, feeling better than she had in a long time. Not even Mackenzie could change that by sending her memes of people looking shocked or crying. Sloane ignored them, only to have the messages start.

Mackenzie: **Got anything for me Sloane-y?**

Sloane: **Shut up, Tootie.**

Mackenzie: **You'll be sorry tomorrow. Get ready for a Mac Attack.**

After that, Sloane blocked her. Because Slayer Sloane had made a decision. She was going to tell Amelia everything. Nothing Mackenzie did was going to change that.

In the morning, Sloane once again got to school early, her stomach queasy with nerves. The way it always got right before a big match.

"SLOANE!" a familiar, overly emotional voice cried from the other end of the hallway. "Sloane, Sloane, Sloane, Sloane, *Sloane*!"

Amelia grabbed Sloane by the arm and dragged her into the bathroom.

"Hey, I've got to talk to you," Sloane began, only to get a good look at Amelia. "Why are you wearing that?"

For the first time that Sloane could remember, Amelia was wearing jeans and a hoodie like any normal person. Which on Amelia was totally weird.

"I'm going incognito." She also had on a pair of sunglasses, which she took off and stuffed into her curls so she could see Sloane better. "You will *not* believe what I found out last night!"

"Yeah, hey. Before we get to that, I have something I have to tell you—"

"I'm Thomas Zimmerman's great-great-granddaughter!" Amelia cried out. Immediately, her eyes widened in horror. Scurrying about, she checked under the stalls to make sure no one else was listening.

Stunned, Sloane gasped, *"What?"*

"My mom helped put it all together!" Amelia continued, tears welling up in her eyes. "Her dad was Johnny Kerr, who was Oscar Kerr's son. He went to prison for robbery right around the time my mom was born. I'm from a long line of criminals, Sloane! I never minded being weird before—well, okay, I did—but I always thought that someday I'd graduate and find people just like me. Creative people! Interesting people! But instead, my actual people are *criminals*. Sloane, I don't want to be a criminal!"

"Amelia! Calm down." Sloane patted her friend's shoulder awkwardly, wishing her grannies were here. She wasn't really great at comforting people, but what would Granny Pearl and Granny Kitty do?

Probably stuff food at her.

Sloane dragged Amelia out of the bathroom and down to the cafeteria, where she bought the other girl a package of Pop-Tarts. They settled down at one of the cafeteria tables, as far away from the other breakfast kids as they could.

Amelia stuffed a Pop-Tart into her mouth, tears trickling down her cheeks. Thickly, she explained, "They're all awful, my whole family! Charles figured out that Oscar had the jewels but couldn't prove it at first. He begged my great-grandfather Oscar to give him the money to save his daughter's life. She was dying and had a kid, and he just wanted the money to treat her cancer. But my great-grandfather wouldn't give it to him! What kind of a monster does something like that? Maybe everyone in my family is just made wrong. Maybe that's why everyone makes fun of me. They know deep down that I'm bad. They can feel it in their bones."

"What? No!" Sloane reassured her. Then she remembered the telegram she'd come across last night from Spade Investigators and put the pieces together. "And Amelia, Oscar wouldn't give Charles the money because the treatment for his daughter was a complete scam. There was a letter from a detective that Oscar hired to find out about it. The treatment was arsenic."

Amelia stopped snuffling and paused with a pastry halfway to her mouth. "What, like the poison?"

"*Exactly* like the poison." Sloane nodded vigorously. "I looked it up, and apparently medicine used to be pretty scary. You could say that all sorts of things were good for you or would cure stuff. Did you know that *cigarettes* were even advertised as being good for you?"

"Ugh. Gross." Amelia made a face. Then she laid her Pop-Tart back down on its wrapper. "My great-grandfather was trying to protect Charles?"

"He was definitely trying to protect Charles," Sloane reassured the other girl. "Who knows? Maybe he was planning on giving all of the jewels back to Charles eventually. As of May eleventh, 1940, Charles's daughter must have still been alive because that was the date on the letter from the detectives, warning Oscar not to give Charles any money."

"Charles's daughter's name was Lucy, and she was dead by October eighth, 1940, because that was the date on the first letter threatening Oscar." By now, Amelia had perked up quite a bit. She wiped the tears from her face with the sleeve of her hoodie. "It's still not great that my great-grandfather sold jewels that he knew were stolen. But he *did* think that Charles was super rich and didn't need the money."

"And by the time he found out that Charles had lost all of his money, he couldn't hand over the jewels or Charles would have just wasted them on arsenic that would've killed his daughter even more quickly than the cancer," Sloane continued as the warning bell rang. In five minutes, they would be tardy. The few other kids still in the cafeteria picked up their trays and tossed them into the garbage.

Sloane and Amelia got up too but walked as slowly as they could toward class, keeping their heads together and their voices down. Amelia picked up where Sloane had left off a minute before. "And then Charles and Oscar were both dead soon after. Oscar from his accident with the streetcar and Charles dead from—I don't know. Arsenic? Heartbreak, maybe? And we still don't know what baby we're supposed to be looking for, let alone how to find it."

"Ugh. It's all so pointless and sad." Sloane made a face. She filled Amelia in on the snotty letter Jacob had sent Thomas, offering him a crappy job instead of the cash. "Jacob was a real jerk. Thomas gave him money to start up his business, but Jacob was convinced it was a gift, not a loan that he was supposed to pay back."

"Maybe he misunderstood," Amelia pointed out, seeming to feel quite perky and generous now that she knew she wasn't related to a guy who had let someone die because of greed. "I mean, these guys weren't exactly great communicators, were they? Jacob didn't want to listen to Thomas about how he needed money. Thomas didn't tell his wife he was going to rob Jacob until after it had already happened. Beatrice didn't tell her son about the jewels until she was about to die. Oscar never told his family *anything*, and Charles didn't want to listen when he found out that the 'medicine' for his daughter was really poison. Between all of the not-telling and not-listening, who knows what anyone's motives were or what really happened? Oh, hey. And speaking of telling people things, what did you want to tell me?"

Having just reached Mr. Roth's door, Amelia screeched to a halt. Her face was still a bit blotchy, but she looked like her old self now. Well, minus the normal clothes she was wearing. She waited expectantly, eyes all big and shiny, certain that Sloane had something exciting to say.

Which, Sloane definitely did.

And there was no way she could say it.

Not right now, not after Amelia had been crying, only to get cheered up by Sloane. It would be just too cruel to tell her.

"Um, just what I found out about the arsenic," Sloane said faintly, pulling at her ponytail. "And Jacob being a jerk. That's pretty much it."

She'd tell Amelia tomorrow. Yes, definitely tomorrow. Today she'd have to bribe Mackenzie somehow. Maybe she could get her dad to give Mac a discount on her retainer?

However, as they stepped into Mr. Roth's classroom, the decision on what to tell Amelia and when slid right out of Sloane's hands.

Because a bunch of kids were looking at their phones and giggling. When Sloane and Amelia walked in, Kylee and Mylie snickered all the harder. Schroeder looked at both of them, shook his head, and walked away. Some of the other kids did as well.

But a few stayed, still laughing and forming a half circle around Mackenzie.

Who smiled sweetly at Amelia and said, "Hey, Yeti! Ever wondered where your nickname came from? Ever wondered who came up with it?"

Before Sloane could stop her, Mac held up her phone. The video of Easter Bunny Sloane saying, "She's like a yeti herself. A hairy, weird, dramatic yeti. Amelia the Yeti!" played before launching into some dance music with Sloane repeating over and over again, "Yeti! Yeti! Yeti!"

Amelia snatched the phone out of Mackenzie's hand and gaped at it as Mac smirked. The pit of Sloane's stomach dropped all the way into her knees, making them wobble.

This couldn't be happening.

"Sloane?" Amelia dropped Mackenzie's phone like it had burned her. She turned huge, watery eyes onto her friend.

Onto the person she'd *thought* was her friend.

"I'm so sorry," Sloane whispered. She was Amelia's friend. She *was*. "Amelia, I—"

Amelia didn't care what Sloane had to say.

She turned and ran right out of the classroom.

Amelia wasn't a monster, no matter what her relatives might or might not have done.

Unfortunately, Sloane sure felt like one right now.

13

ALL ALONE

Having a family who constantly tells you all of the things that are wrong with you can be very unlucky. However, even bad luck frequently brings good luck along with it. In Amelia's case, it meant that no matter how much kids at school teased her about being a yeti, it was still better than all the criticism she got at home. True, it hurt her feelings very badly, but it never once made the slightest dent in her determination to be herself somewhere.

Because Amelia knew she wasn't a yeti. Now, however, Amelia suddenly felt like she knew something else about herself. It wasn't true, but neither good luck nor bad luck could be blamed for Amelia believing it.

What she now believed was that she was a fool.

A stupid, stupid, worthless fool. Who had actually believed that a Cool Person like Sloane could like some weirdo like her.

After she fled the classroom, Amelia didn't stop running until she reached the office.

"I need to go home," she told Ms. Joan, the secretary.

Then she threw up all over the office counter.

Normally, Miller-Poes were not allowed to go home sick. Their parents (and older siblings) told them to tough it out because Miller-Poes were not quitters.

However, not even Amanda Poe and Judge Alexander Miller could argue with a big pile of vomit. And a principal and school secretary eager to get Amelia out of there before another pile showed up.

Soon enough, Amelia found herself at home, tucked into her big, sparkling white bed in her big, sparkling white room. It felt rather like being in a hospital, to be honest. There couldn't be many hospital rooms that were cleaner than this one, that was for certain.

"You don't have a temperature." Her mom frowned at the thermometer she'd just taken out of Amelia's mouth. She regarded Amelia the way she always did: as a problem to be solved. "It must be the protein shake Aiden gave you for breakfast this morning. I told you it would make you sick."

"It's not the protein shake." Miserably, Amelia wished her mom would go away and leave her in peace. Well, miserable peace, anyhow.

"It's too rich for your stomach," Amanda Poe continued as though Amelia hadn't said anything at all. She forced Amelia to lean forward so she could stuff another pillow behind her. Even though Amelia had already told her she didn't want another one. "I'll go get you some saltines."

"I don't want any saltines."

"Then, once you've rested, we'll go for a jog," her mom decided, giving the pillows a whack. "We'll settle your tummy down and then give you a boost of endorphins with a run. You'll be ready to go back to school by lunchtime!"

What? No! No way. Amelia was not going back to school for the rest of the year. Not with Traitor Sloane there, laughing at her behind her back. Boy, had she been a fool believing that a cool person like Sloane could be her friend. She should have known it was all one big, cruel prank so Sloane and Mackenzie could have a laugh at her.

"I have consumption," Amelia announced, flopping back against the too-big pile of pillows.

"What on earth is consumption?" her mom demanded impatiently.

"Something that people used to die of back in Victorian times. I've got it, and I'm definitely going to die of it!" A sob tore from Amelia's throat. She couldn't stand the way her mom was looking at her any longer, so she turned around and buried her face in the pillows.

Maybe if she was lucky, she'd suffocate to death.

Then everyone would be sorry.

"Amelia?" The pillows muffled the sound of her mom's voice. "Is this about my father? About your grandfather?"

"I don't know, Mom! Why don't you tell me?" Amelia burst out, rolling over.

"What?" Her mom drew her hand back in shock.

"Why are you asking me? You never ask me anything. *None* of you ever asks me anything! You just tell me what I'm feeling, what I'm thinking, and what I should be doing," Amelia ranted, bunching the edge of the blankets up in her fists. "All of you—Dad, Aiden, Ashley, you! I'm the one who knows what's wrong with me. And *no one* can fix it!"

Unable to face the world one second longer, Amelia dove under the comforter and curled up into the tightest ball she possibly could.

Maybe if she squeezed hard enough, she'd compress herself down into a singular point and the universe would collapse around her.

Ha. Like she'd ever be that lucky.

"Amelia?" Her mom jabbed at the blankets, trying to find her. Wait, no—not jabbing. Was her mom trying to pat her? Like a comforting pat?

That couldn't possibly be right.

"Amelia—I'm . . . sorry." Amanda Poe tripped over the words. They were clearly as foreign to her as a different language. She tried again, more convincingly. "I'm really sorry if I've done something to upset you. Can you tell me about it?"

Slowly, suspiciously, Amelia emerged from the blankets. She squinted her eyes at her mom. "I don't know. Can you listen? Without telling me what's wrong or what I should do?"

Amanda Poe opened her mouth, clearly ready to protest. Amelia narrowed her eyes further, and her mom swallowed back whatever she'd been about to say. In a slightly strangled voice, she said, "I can try."

At least that was an honest answer.

"It's not just you and Dad and Aiden and Ashley, Mom. It's a lot of things." Amelia sighed. "But it doesn't help that I can't talk with you guys about things."

"You can talk with us about anything!"

"No, Mom, I can't. You talk *at* me and to me and around me. Never *with* me."

"Oh."

Silence hung in the air between them. Amelia looked at her

mom, hoping that her mom had finally heard her but not able to believe she really had. Finally, Amanda Poe managed to say, "Why don't we go downstairs and eat some cookies? And I'll . . . try to listen."

Her mom didn't eat cookies. Not ever.

Or at the very least, not that Amelia knew about. Having followed her mom down to their too-big, sparkling kitchen, she watched as her mom rooted out a box of pastries from Sully's from the very back of the pantry. All the way back behind the pasta maker no one ever used. Amanda Poe set them down on the too-big island, and then to Amelia's complete bafflement, she went on to make them hot chocolate as well.

Maybe her mom was having some sort of stroke. Should she call for an ambulance? Amelia wondered.

With the cocoa made, they both climbed up into chairs at the island. For the first time ever for Amelia, the kitchen didn't seem too big. Or maybe it was that the distance between her and her family finally felt a bit smaller.

Maybe.

Hesitantly, Amelia told her mom about everything that had happened with Sloane—and about everything before that, too. About being called a yeti for the last month and everyone thinking it was hilarious. About not wanting to tell her family because then it would be like she was the Yeti at school *and* at home because everyone would insist on telling her what to do.

About how they always treated her like a problem.

Miraculously, her mom listened. It had to be very, *very* hard for Amanda Poe. Amelia could tell by the way her mom would straighten up, open her mouth, and then cram a cookie into it or pour hot chocolate down her throat to keep herself from saying anything.

Still her mom did it, and when Amelia was done talking, she just said, "I'm sorry, honey. This must all be terribly hard for you."

"Yeah, it is." Amelia picked at her cookie, remembering this past weekend when she'd eaten cookies with Sloane. When she'd felt like she was finally being accepted for who she was.

"That Sloane is the worst."

"The absolute worst." Amelia could feel tears welling up in her eyes. She didn't want Sloane to be the worst. She wanted the other girl to be who Amelia thought she was: her friend.

"What would you like me to do?" her mom asked. Amelia gaped at her.

"You're *asking* me?"

"Yes, and it's very hard for me to do," Amanda Poe said in a slightly shrill voice. "So, if you know what you want, you might want to tell me."

"I just want *this*, Mom. To be able to tell you and to have you agree that it stinks. That's mostly all I want." Amelia thought for a moment. "Oh, and I'd *really* like out of Miller-Poe sports nights."

"Absolutely not. Exercise is good for you and family time is important," her mom snapped in her decision-making, financial-advisor, this-is-what's-good-for-you voice. Then, catching herself, she immediately added, "But . . . maybe two nights a week we could all do what *you* want to do. And it doesn't have to be a sport. We could even watch old movies like you used to do with Grandma Suzy. Deal?"

"Deal."

Her mom also agreed to let Amelia stay at home for the rest of the day, though Amanda Poe had to get back to work. Amelia watched her mom go, mind reeling. She couldn't remember the last time she'd talked to her mom like that. She'd sort of assumed that being miserable was the only way she could live her life. That no one would really listen to her if she tried to tell them what she was thinking.

Then Sloane had come along and treated her like a real person, and Amelia had liked how that felt. Together, they'd accomplished things no one else had in more than a hundred years.

Even if Sloane's friendship had been fake, the clues they'd uncovered weren't. In a weird way, in spite of everything, that gave Amelia the confidence to believe she could change her life. Right now. She didn't have to wait until she was grown up.

So, Amelia decided to continue making changes. Starting with figuring out where those missing jewels were. Having made sure that her mom had driven off, Amelia marched upstairs and traded her pajamas for her trench coat and brimmed hat. With the hat pulled down to hide her identity, Amelia walked to the Fulton County Historical Museum. It was actually quite hot and sunny out, so the coat only made it halfway there before Amelia slung it over her shoulder. She kept the hat on, though, so she was at least half a private investigator.

The lilac tree leaning against the porch was in full purply bloom when she got there. There were also several people Amelia hadn't expected: Mr. Neikirk, Meredith, and Ty. They were all carrying huge boxes up the steps. Well, Ty was trying. Mostly he was getting stuck in the lilac tree.

"Here, let me help you." Amelia untangled Ty's sweater from the branches that had grabbed it. "What's going on?"

"Grampy is donating the worthless junk from the estate sale over on Oak Street to the museum," Ty explained. At the words "worthless junk," Mr. Neikirk whipped his head around. Ty flushed and hastily corrected, "I mean, we're generously donating some important historical artifacts to the museum."

Hopping up and down, Amelia tried to get a good look at what was in the box. As far as she could tell, "worthless junk" seemed about right. The "important historical artifacts" included a lot of water-stained magazines from the 1950s and an ancient blender with the sort of frayed electrical cable that seemed like it might come in handy if you wanted to electrocute someone.

Inside the museum, Milton appeared positively distraught to be receiving Mr. Neikirk's "donations." He was so upset that he accidentally grabbed a Slytherin mug and poured coffee into it. "But Mr. Neikirk, the museum doesn't need any of this!"

"Too bad! Dumping stuff at the landfill costs money, and I can write this off on my taxes!" the tiny man chirped. "Say, you wouldn't want to sell that stuffed owl, would you? I know someone who'd pay good money for it."

"You can't have Hedwig!" Milton gasped. Looking down, he realized he was holding a silver-and-green mug rather than a scarlet-and-gold one. He yelped and dropped it, spattering coffee onto his shirt and desk.

"Yeah, I'm not having the greatest day, either." Amelia patted him on his arm as Mr. Neikirk continued to poke around the museum, shouting out values like he wanted Ty and Meredith to start slapping stickers on things. To distract an obviously upset Milton, Amelia asked, "How'd you end up with a Slytherin mug, anyhow?"

"Joke gift from my brother." Milton tugged morosely at his bow tie. "He thinks he's so funny. Have you seen my Gryffindor mug? It's got to be around here somewhere."

As Amelia helped the museum curator search the room, Belinda walked in. She had Bunny at her side and a stack of large dusty books in her hands.

"Not much value in those," Mr. Neikirk clucked, shaking his head. "Now, that motorcycle of yours out there . . ."

"Not for sale," Belinda told him firmly. When the auctioneer's eyes slid to Bunny, she added, "Him either."

Amelia would have hidden under Milton's desk to keep the librarian from spotting her, since Belinda was the person most likely to realize she should be in school. However, Mr. Neikirk's boxes of junk blocked her escape route. Still, Amelia tried it all the same, only to knock one of them over. She grabbed it to keep it from falling, but Milton's Gryffindor mug tipped out of it anyhow. It bounced against Amelia's nose, giving the curator enough time to grab it.

"Thank goodness you rescued it!" Milton hugged the ceramic mug.

Belinda took the box out of Amelia's hands, but considered her beadily. "Hey, shouldn't you be in school?"

"Special circumstances," Amelia said, her voice embarrassingly thick. Bunny seemed to sense something was wrong and leaned reassuringly against her side. Amelia ran her hands over his fur and felt a little better.

For once, Belinda gave in to her biker side rather than her librarian side and went off to scold Mr. Neikirk about the careless way he was treating some of the antique books.

Pulling herself together, Amelia asked Milton, "Could you help me look someone up? Someone who would have been born about a hundred years ago?"

"Sure!" Milton enthused, going over to his laptop. "The museum pays for subscriptions to all sorts of genealogy databases. Who are you trying to find?"

"I'm looking for Charles Hoäl's daughter." Amelia peered over his shoulder as Bunny went off to hang out with Ty and Meredith in the foyer on the steps to the creepy upstairs.

The museum curator tapped away furiously at the keyboard. "Um, according to the US census, he was married by 1910 to a Rebecca Schmitt. And by 1920, they also had a little girl named Lucy, age eight. So that means she would have been born in 1912."

Lucy Hoäl, born 1912. Amelia added a note to her phone. Charles had talked about his darling Lucy having a baby of her own before she died. "Any way to see if Lucy ever had a kid?"

"Um. Hmm. Let's see if she got married first." Milton did a bit more tapping. "Okay—it looks like Lucy Hoäl married a Henry Mohr around 1933 and had a baby girl named Charlotte in 1934.

And—oh, this is sad—there's a death certificate for Lucy in 1940."

Charlotte had been six when her mother died. Not exactly a baby, but try to tell a parent or grandparent that. Amanda Poe still sometimes referred to Amelia as her "baby" and so did Grandma Suzy.

"When did Charlotte die?" Amelia asked, laying down her phone.

Milton did a bit more searching of birth and death certificates before frowning and saying, "Looks like she hasn't. She got married in 1955, though, to a Robert Yoder here in Wauseon. Does that help at all?"

"I'm not sure," Amelia admitted. "Does she still live anywhere around here?"

"Eighty-two Leggett Street. Hey, do you think you know where the missing jewels are, then?" Milton asked, eyes big. "Wow! Gosh, can you imagine finding them after all this time?"

Amelia could, actually.

However, before she could say so, Belinda returned with the book Mr. Neikirk had been manhandling. The auctioneer tagged after her, harrumphing, "What are you so worried about? Wouldn't get ten dollars for it at auction!"

"It has important information in it!" Belinda shot back in outrage, before turning to Milton and Amelia. "And speaking of important information, you guys really need to tell Mr. Roth about this! I bet he's dying to find out where those jewels are."

"Who wouldn't be?" Mr. Neikirk's eyes brightened as he considered Amelia. "Whoever finds them will be fabulously rich."

Maybe. Amelia didn't mention the fact that at least some of the jewels had already been sold off. Clearly not all of them, or Charles never would have been able to torment Oscar with his scavenger hunt.

Besides, Amelia had just noticed someone out on the sidewalk.

Someone on a bike.

Someone who was tugging at her ponytail.

Someone who should most definitely *not* be here.

"Excuse me." Before Milton, Belinda, or Mr. Neikirk could say anything, Amelia dashed through the foyer, past a startled Ty and Meredith, and outside with her fists clenched. She marched up to Sloane and demanded, "What are you doing here? How did you know I was here?"

"Amelia! I've been looking for you everywhere!" Sloane hopped off her bike.

"Oh, I'm 'Amelia' now, am I?" Tears sprang into Amelia's eyes. "Not 'the Yeti'?"

Sloane at least had the decency to look so sick that Amelia thought, for a moment, she might throw up. Amelia might have felt bad about that had she not *actually* thrown up earlier that day.

"I've got to talk to you," Sloane managed.

"Shouldn't you be at school?"

"Yeah, I should. But I'm cutting class. And I'm totally going to get into major trouble for that," Sloane added. "But look, I'm really, *really* sorry, Amelia. I *so* am. Like, majorly, incredibly sorry."

She looked so sad and anxious standing there, pulling at her hair, that Amelia almost believed her—almost. What stopped Amelia was how badly she *wanted* to believe that Sloane really was sorry. Even more than finding the lost Cursed Hoäl Treasure, the thing that Amelia wanted more than anything in the world was to have a friend.

To know that there was someone who knew how weird she was and liked her because of it.

Which, no doubt, was exactly what Sloane was counting on. Amelia had probably gotten it wrong and the other girl didn't tug on her hair when she was nervous. She did it when she was fiendishly plotting how to torture people. Right now, maybe she was filming this whole thing with her camera so all of the other kids at school could laugh at stupid, desperate, pathetic Amelia.

Well, she wasn't stupid or desperate or pathetic. Even if she did have tears stinging her eyes and her skin was all hot and itchy with emotion.

"You're sorry, huh?" Amelia snapped. "What, exactly, are you sorry about? Getting everyone to call me a yeti or the fact that I finally found out that this was all *your* doing?"

Sloane finally let go of her bike, allowing it to fall into the grass. "Amelia, I swear it wasn't! It was that day at the library when you started talking about my mom. And I was so mad and sad when you left that it just came out. I never thought anyone else would think it was so funny. I swear—I swear—I swear on my mom's memory that I never meant for any of this to happen."

The other girl's voice caught in her throat as she spoke. This time, Amelia was pretty sure she believed Sloane about it all being an accident. A fire that she'd unintentionally started only to have it burn out of control.

That should have made her feel better, but it didn't. It just made her feel sort of empty inside.

"I believe you," Amelia said slowly. "But here's the thing, Sloane: Did you ever try to stop anyone from calling me a yeti?"

Stricken, Sloane didn't say anything. Slowly, she shook her head.

"Yeah, that's what I thought. Maybe you didn't mean to start it . . . but you did. And you didn't do anything to try to fix it, did you?" Amelia could see the truth of her words on her supposed-friend's face. "You just let them keep on teasing me."

That felt like an appropriately dramatic moment to end this conversation. Amelia only wished she had a microphone to drop before doing so. She started to march off down the sidewalk with her head held high . . . only to realize she'd dropped her phone on Milton's desk inside the museum.

Trying to look like she meant to do it, Amelia took a slight U-turn back toward the museum's second, rarely used entrance. Glancing over her shoulder, she saw that Sloane was still watching her with a crushed look on her face. It should have made Amelia feel happy—or at least satisfied. Instead, she just felt sicker and lonelier than ever.

Plus, the door to the second entrance was locked, forcing Amelia to walk all the way back down the porch to the main entrance. By the time she went inside, got her phone, and came back out again, Sloane was gone. Fortunately, Milton, Belinda, Mr. Niekirk, Ty, and Meredith had all moved into other parts of the museum so she didn't have to see them.

Amelia squeezed her hands tightly around her phone, tears welling up in her eyes.

She'd found a friend, only to lose her.

Just like her great-great-grandfather had. Just like her great-grandfather had.

Maybe she would have been luckier never to have had a friend at all.

14

SLOANE ALMOST DROPS THE MIC

Right at that point in time, it was unlikely that the Missing Hoäl Treasure (or Cursed Hoäl Treasure, depending on your opinion) would ever be found. However, the person who had started it all would have been just fine with that. That person was practically cackling with glee over the amount of information Sloane and Amelia had already found. If the two girls never made up, that would just be two fewer obstacles in need of removing.

Sloane, however, was not just fine with things. That evening, she lay on her stomach across her bed, scowling at her concrete goose in its *Doctor Who* costume on the floor. It seemed sympathetic but didn't have much to say.

She was in quite a bit of trouble for cutting school. Not only did she have after-school detention for a week, her dad had left work to find her, leaving some poor kid with his mouth still pried open. Nanna Tia had shut down her illegal bingo operation, kicking a bunch of gambling-crazed senior citizens out of her house. Plus, Grannies Pearl and Kitty had power-walked all over town, looking for her.

In fact, they were the ones who found her, sitting on her bike in North Park by the Civil War monument. They hustled her home and tried to feed her ice cream. Then when that didn't work, soup.

Sloane didn't want any of it. She wanted . . . she wanted . . .

Well, what she wanted was a time machine like the TARDIS. That was what she wanted. So she could go back to that day a month ago and fix things.

"Hey there, Slayer." Her dad poked his head into her room. "Mind if I come in?"

Sloane grunted and shrugged her shoulders, her mouth and nose buried in a pillow.

Her dad flopped onto the bed next to her and stared at the goose too. "Want to tell me about what happened today?"

"I'm a horrible person."

"I don't think that's true."

"You're my dad; by law you're not allowed to think that I'm a horrible person."

"I don't think that's true, either." Her dad smiled at her but Sloane just scowled harder.

"It *is* true," she snapped, sitting upright. "Or at least, it's true that *some* of the time I'm a horrible person."

"Oh, Sloane." Sighing, her dad sat up too. "We're all terrible people some of the time. The important thing is that you don't like it when you are. And that you try really hard not to act that way again. That's how we all become better people."

He gave her a kiss on the head and left her alone to think. Which Sloane did, and the more she did, she realized that Amelia was probably scared to trust her again. Saying "I'm sorry" is easy enough, for all that people act like it isn't. Doing what her dad had just said—acting differently—took time and a lot of hard work.

Sloane didn't mind hard work, but she didn't have a whole lot of time. Whoever had sent them those letters was probably looking for the Hoäl treasure too. Even if they weren't, she and Amelia still needed to work together to finish the project. Sloane needed to—Sloane needed to . . .

Oh. Sloane just thought of something she could do. She didn't *need* to, exactly. But she *could* do it.

It wasn't a great plan. In fact, when she thought about it too much, Sloane had to admit it was a pretty awful plan.

But she was going to do it just the same.

First thing Thursday morning the entire seventh grade gathered in the gym for their annual club and sports assembly. This was a yearly rite of passage in which kids were forced onto the bleachers in the gym so they could watch other kids get certificates for being in band or football or whatever. Anyone who hadn't taken part in some sort of activity got to feel left out. Anyone who *had* taken part in an activity got to slink down onto the gym floor with their shoulders hunched while praying that no one laughed at them.

As a member of the volleyball team, the softball team, *and* the band, Sloane would normally be doing a lot of praying that morning.

However, Sloane was pretty sure she wasn't going to make it through the entire assembly.

She was also fairly certain that the detentions she'd received for leaving school early without permission yesterday weren't going to be her last detentions. In fact, she'd probably start eighth grade with a whole bunch of them left over from this year.

Amelia had returned to school this morning dressed in a long black dress and a hat with a veil. Of course, the other kids had thought that was hilarious, though they'd managed to hide most of their laughter from the teachers. All of the seventh grade was spread out in the bleachers, clustering together by groups of friends. Amelia sat alone, head held high for all that the other kids were whispering about her behind their hands.

Down on the gym floor, underneath the home team basketball net, Principal Stuckey had set up a podium next to a table with boxes of certificates. As always, there seemed to be a struggle to get the microphone to work. Once it was working, there was a further struggle to get it to work *without* the ear-piercing feedback that made all of the kids clap their hands over their ears.

Finally, the assembly began. First, they honored fall sports and clubs alphabetically.

Cross-country went up.

Then football.

Math Counts.

Power of the Pen.

Quiz Bowl.

And finally, volleyball.

When the other girls got up to get their certificates, Sloane made sure she was last. Everyone else had already gotten theirs and were now lined up along the foul-shot line when Sloane reached Principal Stuckey.

As the principal handed Sloane her certificate, Sloane displayed the reflexes that had gotten her the nickname "Slayer" and swiped the microphone. "Hey, mind if I borrow this for a moment?"

"What? No!" However, Principal Stuckey had been out of the classroom too long to be used to dealing with misbehaving students. Sloane had the microphone in her hand before the principal realized it.

"Thanks. I'll bring it right back." Sloane was already booking it down to the other end of the gym, talking quickly into the microphone as she went. "I've got something to say to the entire seventh-grade class, and since we're all stuck here, I'm gonna say it now: we're all jerks."

Wow. She really had everyone's attention, which was not exactly where Sloane had ever wanted to be. Still, she'd brought this on herself and she was going to see it through to the end. Which was probably going to be *really* soon, given that Mr. Roth and two other teachers were already headed in her direction.

Making the most of the time she had, Sloane looked steadily at the entire seventh-grade class, most of whom were gaping at her. Even Amelia had her mouth hanging open. "Yeah, you heard me. We're all jerks. Me, you, the kids sitting next to you—and definitely Mackenzie Snyder."

"What?" Mackenzie's eyes bugged out.

Sloane had to hustle back to the other end of the gym to avoid the teachers now circling her. That put her right by Mac. "You heard me, I said you're a jerk." Now Mac tried to giggle to show how stupid Sloane was being, but everyone else was still too stunned to join her. "But I'm the biggest jerk of all. And given my competition, that's saying something." Sloane used her thumb to jab in Mackenzie's direction. Now some kids *did* laugh, but they were definitely laughing at Mac, not Sloane. Mackenzie's laughter stopped as she crossed her arms and scowled.

In the bleachers, Amelia was sitting up straighter, watching Sloane with distrustful eyes.

Sloane really hoped she was doing the right thing.

Turning to face Principal Stuckey, Sloane confessed, "About a month ago, I called Amelia a yeti behind her back because I was angry with her. Then Mackenzie over here turned it into a meme and sent it to half the volleyball team. And then *they* sent it to people and those people sent it to people, and well, you get the idea."

She'd had to circle around the team to avoid the teachers trying to get the microphone away from her. Not surprisingly, none of the team looked particularly happy with Sloane.

At least they also looked a little ashamed too, Sloane thought.

"And I don't think any of us really meant to bully Amelia, exactly. It was just something everyone thought was funny— but no one ever stopped to think about how it must be making Amelia feel. But I did, and I could tell it was hurting her feelings, and I just stood there and did nothing." To avoid Mr. Roth, Sloane jogged back to the center of the gym, forcing her to face everyone, including Amelia. Sloane looked straight at her former friend and said, "Amelia, I told myself that I was better than everyone else because at least I never called you a yeti after that first time. But that's garbage because I could see how much it was hurting you. So, at least in my opinion, that makes me the biggest jerk of everyone. Because I knew it was wrong, and I didn't do anything to help."

There, she'd done it. For the rest of her school career, she'd probably be known as Sloane the Snitch rather than Slayer Sloane because she'd gotten everyone in trouble. However, at least now all of the teachers knew to be listening for the word "yeti" so they could stop things if anyone tried to call Amelia that again.

Not that anyone was likely to be making fun of her for a while. If there was anyone they were going to target, it was definitely going to be Sloane.

What Amelia was thinking, Sloane didn't have time to figure out. For she'd stayed in one place too long, allowing Mr. Roth to finally catch up with her.

Trying to wrestle the microphone out of her hands, he announced into it, "Thank you, Sloane, for that, uh, unexpected speech. It sounds like we will be having some discussions in homeroom the next couple of weeks about bullying and treating each other with kindness and respect, but—"

He almost had the microphone out of her hands, but Sloane managed to wrench it back one last time. "Forget the discussions! Just don't be rude to each other! I know it's kinda a relief when someone else is getting picked on because it means *you're* safe, but how about if we're all just not rude to each other? How about that, Mackenzie? Huh? *How about just not being rude?*"

Whatever Mackenzie might have had to say to that, Sloane never found out. Because Mr. Roth ripped the microphone out of her hand and the other two teachers hustled her out of the gym. Which was too bad.

She'd sort of been hoping she could drop the mic and walk away.

Yup, it turned out you could have detentions that carried over from one year to the next. Sloane wondered if maybe she could talk her dad into switching schools before eighth grade started.

Because she probably was not going to be super popular around here for a while. The whole grade had to take part in antibullying activities between now and the summer break. Even worse (or better, depending on your point of view), Mackenzie was going to be in detention with her too, for showing the video at school.

"I'll get you for this," Mackenzie threatened as they left the office together later that morning.

Sloane turned to her and said, "Mac, I just humiliated myself in front of the entire seventh grade and got everyone assigned to bullying prevention classes for the rest of the school year. What do you think you can do to top that?"

Mackenzie opened and closed her mouth several times, clearly trying to come up with *something* to top that. And failing. In the end, she settled on snapping, "Yeah? Well, at least *I* still have friends. Enjoy sitting alone at lunch for the rest of your life."

Ugh. Sloane winced as Mackenzie stomped off. Mac

certainly had a talent for identifying a person's weak spot and then sliding the knife right in.

Because she was right. Amelia probably still hated her and everyone else *definitely* did.

Getting in trouble had taken so long that it was already lunchtime. Sloane wondered if Principal Stuckey had planned that on purpose. She would have happily served a year's worth of after-school detentions if it meant avoiding all of the glares she was going to get when she walked into the lunchroom today.

Imagining it, Slayer Sloane decided she'd had enough of being brave for one day. Instead of going to the cafeteria, she slunk off to the farthest bathroom she could find. Shutting herself into one of the stalls, she sat down on the edge of the toilet seat and wished she'd thought to grab her lunch out of her locker. Now she didn't want to go back for fear that she'd run into any of her teachers. Who *might* take mercy on her and let her eat lunch in one of their classrooms. But who might also force her back into the cafeteria because they were done with her nonsense.

"Sloane?" A pair of black Chucks came into the room, followed by the train of a long black dress. Their owner knocked on the closed stall door. "Are you in there?"

Sloane pushed the door open to find Amelia standing there, clutching a fabric lunch bag in her hands. Her eyes were big and shining. Reverently, she whispered, "That was simply amazing. You were like vengeance personified. A goddess of retribution."

"I don't know what that means." Sloane came out of the stall. "But I hope it means that we're friends again."

"You are the loyalest, truest friend anyone could have!" Amelia announced dramatically, squeezing the handles of her lunch sack all the tighter. "Do you want to share my lunch?"

"Oh, yes, please."

Together, they hopped up onto the counter. Amelia dug out her sandwich and handed Sloane half. At first, she thought it was normal peanut butter, only to realize that it was actually peanut butter and pickles. Which seemed like a very Amelia sort of thing to eat.

"I found out that Charles Hoäl's granddaughter is still alive," Amelia told her while they ate their sandwiches.

"What? No way!"

"Yup." Amelia's nodded her head so vigorously that her red curls bounced up and down. "Do you think if we talked to her, she might be able to give us some clues about what Charles meant by that whole 'Find the baby, find the jewels' message?"

"It's worth a try," Sloane said. Unlike peanut-butter-and-pickle sandwiches, which were definitely *not* worth a try. Not that she was going to tell Amelia that.

"One thing, though" Amelia continued, frowning at her sandwich. "I'd still really like to know who sent us those letters, and why. Thirteen million dollars is a lot of motivation to do terrible things to people."

Sloane reached for Amelia's lunch bag to see what else was in there aside from peanut-butter-and-pickle sandwiches. "I always thought it was completely unfair that Mr. Roth was trying to drag in history when he teaches English class. Maybe it isn't just unfair— maybe it's downright evil."

"All along this has been part of his dastardly plan to betray us!" Amelia exclaimed, hopping down off her sink. "But he's also pretty nice, too, for a teacher. I hope if someone is setting us up, it isn't him. I bet it's Principal Stuckey. The graveyard is on her farm, and she always seems to be mysteriously around when things are happening."

"It could be that Neikirk guy." Sloane found some carrots and hummus. "From what you said, he's always finding all sorts of odd things when he clears out people's houses. I think he'd be clever enough to plant the idea in Mr. Roth's head."

"He's definitely very good at manipulating people," Amelia said darkly.

"The trouble is, there's no way we can know who, exactly, came up with the idea for this project. We can't ask Mr. Roth because we won't know if he's telling the truth or not." Sloane scowled and picked up a carrot to crunch on in frustration.

"It could even be Belinda," Amelia pointed out. "Though she does seem more likely to beat someone with a book to find out where the jewels are than to do something like this."

"Or maybe it's Milton!" Sloane suggested. Then she and Amelia looked at each other and burst out laughing. "Okay, probably not Milton. But yeah, you're right. There are a lot of people it could be. Until we've found out who, no more posting videos on YouTube."

"I think you're right." Amelia sighed regretfully as the bell rang. Tossing their trash in the garbage, she grabbed her lunch bag and then they both headed out of the bathroom.

"Oh, hey. You never told me where we can find Charles Hoäl's granddaughter," Sloane said as they walked toward their lockers, other kids filtering into the far end of the hallway.

"That's right." Amelia pulled out her phone to check her notes. "Her name is Charlotte Yoder and she lives at 82 Leggett Street."

Sloane froze in place, unable to believe what she'd just heard. Amelia walked several steps beyond Sloane before she realized that fact. Turning around, she stared at her friend. "Sloane, are you okay? What's wrong? Are you going to pass out? You look like you're going to pass out."

"D-did you just say Charlotte Yoder at 82 Leggett Street?" Sloane finally managed to say, the world around her going blurry at its edges.

"Yeah, why?"

"That's my Nanna Tia's house. My Great-Grandma Charlotte. 'Tia' is her nickname." Sloane's mouth had a hard time forming the words.

"No. Way." Amelia's eyes were huge.

"Yes."

"You're not—"

"I am. I'm Jacob Hoäl's Great-great-great-granddaughter."

15

Find the Baby, Find the Jewels

After school, Sloane had to sit through her very first detention. Amelia was not allowed to join her, so she ended up sitting on a bench in front of the school until Sloane got out. Her black dress was super hot in the sun even without the black hat and veil. By the time Sloane dashed out the front doors an hour later, Amelia was so drenched in sweat that her curls couldn't even frizz anymore.

"Hey," Sloane said.

"Hey." Amelia had planned a short speech while waiting for Sloane. As theatrically as she could, she laid a hand upon her heart and announced, "Sloane, it's time to lay to rest the feud between our two families. It's already claimed far too many lives: Thomas's, Jacob's, Lucretia's, Oscar's, and Charles's. Partly this feud can partly be blamed on unbelievable bad luck—beyond bad luck, even—"

"Zemblanity?"

"Yes, that. But it also can be blamed on our ancestors failing to actually talk *and* listen to each other. Just like how you couldn't talk to your dad, and my family wouldn't listen to me." Amelia extended her hand. "By taking my hand and shaking it, you agree that from now on we will actually talk *and* listen to each other. And that neither one of us will seek vengeance for past wrongs committed by either ourselves or our ancestors."

"Sounds good to me." Sloane took Amelia's hand and shook it vigorously. *Ow*—it figured that Slayer Sloane would have a bone-crushing death grip. "Now let's head over to my Nanna Tia's. Do you have a bike?"

"No, but I texted a ride." As she spoke, Aiden pulled up in front of the curb.

"How's the search for the missing jewels coming?" he asked them as he hooked Sloane's bike onto the rack on the back of his sports car. "Have you beat all the competition—er, found out anything more no one else has?"

"Lots," Amelia said.

"*So* much," Sloane agreed.

"That's my sister!" Aiden punched Amelia on the arm. *Ow, again.* What was with these athletic people? Were they like giants and just didn't have a sense of how strong they were?

Sloane's Nanna Tia lived in a long, low 1950s ranch house with lots of pink flamingo lawn ornaments stuck into the garden. There was also quite a bit of noise drifting out of the house from an open window.

"G thirty-eight!"

"B fifty-two!"

"I nineteen!"

"BINGO!"

"What's going on in there?" Aiden asked, leaning across the passenger seat to peer through the open car door as they got out.

Sloane looked pained. "Do you really want to know what a pack of ninety-year-olds do when no one else is around?"

Aiden seemed terrified just thinking about it. He recoiled back into his seat. "Uh, no. Definitely not. Amelia, Ashley will be over to pick you up in about an hour. Sloane, I'll drop your bike off at your house."

As he snapped his seat belt into place and peeled off down the street, Sloane said to Amelia, "Illegal bingo games."

"What's that?"

"That's what's a pack of ninety-year-olds do when no one else is around. Every Tuesday and Thursday afternoon, she runs illegal bingo games to help cover the cost of her winter home down in Florida."

"Illegal?"

"She doesn't have a gambling license, and Dad keeps worrying that the feds are going to find out and raid her house."

"Then I guess we'd better talk to her before she gets arrested."

Sloane rang the doorbell, but rather than some Nanna Tia person, two women Amelia recognized as Sloane's Granny Kitty and Granny Pearl answered the door.

"Sloane-y! Oh, and it's her little friend Amelia!" As Sloane got her cheeks kissed and pinched, Amelia found her head being patted and her own cheeks pinched, too.

"I'm not little!" she protested as they were both dragged inside.

"Of course you aren't!" Granny Pearl bobbed her head in agreement.

"That's the spirit!" Granny Kitty urged.

"Gail, that's the third time you've bingo-ed! Let me see that card!" An elderly man in suspenders and a striped shirt climbed up onto a card table. He attempted to wrench the bingo card out of the gnarled hands of the woman across from him.

"Back off, Edward." She clung to the card with one hand while also pulling out a tiny screwdriver. "I've got my hearing-aid kit tools with me, and I'm not afraid to use them!"

"Excuse us." As one, Grannies Pearl and Kitty turned around and hustled over to break up the brawl.

"Nanna pays them to be bouncers," Sloane explained gloomily. "Dad worries about that, too, but I think they can handle just about anyone. Let's go find Nanna."

They made their way through an enormous room stuffed with card tables and a large number of elderly people. The walls were covered in woven wood and the ceiling appeared to be made of grass, though that couldn't be right.

"She's decorated it like a 1950s tiki lounge," Sloane further explained when she noticed Amelia looking. Amelia suspected that there was a lot about Sloane's Nanna that needed to be explained. The air was very smoky and all of the bingo players drank out of pineapples and coconuts with little umbrellas stuck in them. However, Sloane assured her that no one was actually smoking or drinking alcohol. "The drinks are all fruit juice because the sugar keeps everyone alert while they play. The smoke is from aromatherapy candles to calm everyone down because things can get—er, a bit tense."

"Gail's leaving! That means her card is up for grabs!" a woman in a tie-dyed shirt shrieked. Several retirees jumped up and swooped down on Lucky Gail's table like a pack of vultures. Granny Pearl and Granny Kitty rushed to break up this new fight.

As they reached the patio door, Amelia noticed a familiar face-off in one corner.

Mr. Neikirk.

He wasn't playing bingo like the rest of them, though he had a coconut drink in his hand. He slurped on it as he watched Amelia and Sloane go out the sliding door.

What was he doing here? Amelia wondered uneasily. If he was here for the game, why wasn't he playing? And if he wasn't here for it, was he looking for Amelia and Sloane?

Amelia was just as glad when Sloane slid the glass door shut. At least the maybe-evil auctioneer wasn't likely to try anything with Granny Pearl and Granny Kitty close by.

Nanna Tia was taking a break out on the back porch. Weird green AstroTurf covered the floor, and she was half lying on a wheeled, flowered lounge chair while fanning herself with an enormous straw hat. Even though she wore a brightly colored muumuu-style dress and sunglasses, she looked like a crime boss in a movie.

"Sloane-y!" she cried cheerfully, though she fortunately seemed too tired to pinch anyone's cheeks.

"Nanna!" Sloane gave her a kiss.

"My dogs are barking." Nanna Tia sighed. When Amelia looked at her in confusion, she added, "That means my feet are tired. I'm getting too old for this bingo business."

She wiggled her toes, which had nails painted neon orange. Amelia could imagine that being a crime boss was exhausting at any age, let alone eighty- or ninety-something.

"This is my friend Amelia. We've got some questions about my great-great-grandma and great-great-great-grandpa."

"That's too many 'great's," Great-Granny complained. "Who do you want, again?"

"Your mom and grandpa."

Sloane's great-grandma swept off her sunglasses so she could see the two of them better. Then she patted the wrought-iron bench next to her and said, "Come sit down, and I'll tell you what I can. But I was only six years old when they died, you know."

"Did you know that your great-grandparents were millionaires?" Amelia asked as Nanna Tia poured a coconut juice and handed it to her. Sloane's great-grandma also offered them a half pineapple covered in skewers of cheese, maraschino cherries, and pineapple chunks, but Amelia passed on that. "Only your grandpa lost it all when the stock market crashed in 1929."

"I'm impressed that you know the stock market crashed in 1929." Nanna Tia nodded approvingly. Amelia sat up straighter, trying to look like a hardworking student who knew all sorts of things other kids didn't. She thought she pulled it off pretty well. "I don't know anything about being related to some millionaires, but I do know that Papa always said Granddaddy took it terribly hard when Mama died. She was his only child, you see, and he'd been orphaned himself. He wanted to give her the perfect, happy family he'd never had. When she got cancer, he was desperate to find some cure. But there just wasn't one back then, and so she died. Papa said that Granddaddy died right after of heartbreak."

Amelia and Sloane both opened up their mouths to ask more questions, but before they could, Nanna Tia added, "Of course, he lived long enough to get them to change the name of the cemetery where he'd buried her. It was just a little cemetery on a farm his father used to own, but he wanted to name it to honor her memory."

Amelia and Sloane exchanged a look over Sloane's coconut drink. Sloane said, "What do you mean?"

"Something about Great-Granddaddy having purchased the farm where he'd worked as a kid. The farm family had always buried their loved ones in that cemetery. Maybe my great-granddaddy liked the thought of being the boss of them in death since they'd bossed him around when he was little."

Amelia wasn't sure how you were going to tell people what to do if you were dead and buried. Especially when they were dead and buried too.

"Anyhow, even after he lost all of his money, Granddaddy held on to that farm and some old house that his parents had owned too, Papa said. He sold them all to pay for Mama's cancer treatment when she got sick, but like I said, it didn't do any good. However, when he sold the farm, it was on the condition that Mama was to be buried there along with him and his parents. He also renamed the cemetery after his baby."

Amelia and Sloane exchanged an excited look. Cautiously—afraid to get her hopes up too much—Amelia asked, "His 'baby'?"

"He always called Mama that."

"So . . . he named the cemetery 'Baby Cemetery'?" Amelia asked, perplexed.

She'd never heard of a baby cemetery before, but it sounded super creepy. She wasn't sure she wanted to go digging for treasure there. Actually, she was positive she didn't.

Nanna Tia nodded. "Well, the Hoäls were actually German, you know. So, Granddaddy named it Saugling Cemetery." When Amelia and Sloane still looked confused, she explained. "'Säugling' is German for 'baby.'"

Saugling Cemetery.

Hold on. . . .

That cemetery on Principal Stuckey's farm had been named Saugling Cemetery.

Right where Mr. Roth had first given them this assignment.

"'Find the baby, find the jewels,'" Amelia repeated. "Sloane, *they were there all along!*"

Sloane looked like someone had clubbed her over the head. "Amelia, I stood next to a tombstone with a baby on it! I thought it was a cupid missing its wings, but now I'm sure it was a baby. And it said 'Lucy'! I thought it said 'Lucky' and that the 'k' had just eroded away!"

"Yes, that's Mama's grave," Nanna Tia confirmed.

Amelia collapsed backward against the bench, unable to say anything more. Sloane joined her, both of them stunned.

They'd been standing right over the jewels when all of this began.

Now that they knew where the jewels were hidden, they had to find a way to get to them. Preferably without whoever had sent those letters following them. They couldn't let Principal Stuckey know what they planned to do, even though the cemetery was on her property. If she was the one who'd set this whole thing up, who knew what she'd do to them? Both Amelia and Sloane were pretty sure that getting put into after-school detention would be the least of their worries.

That meant that they'd need to sneak out there when no one would see them. Possibly in the middle of the night, though neither Sloane nor Amelia was exactly excited about that idea. Fortunately, the cemetery was on the other side of the woods from Principal's Stuckey's house. If they could get out there, they could be fairly sure that she wouldn't see them even in the middle of the day. Less fortunately, her farm was a solid three miles outside of town. That was a long distance to walk through farm fields and woods and across ditches and creeks.

After school (and after Sloane's detention) the next day, the two of them walked to Sloane's house. Once there, they changed into old flannel shirts and jeans that belonged to Sloane. Amelia had to roll up the cuffs on hers by quite a bit. Then they called an Uber and went outside to stand along the leafy curb. They had shovels in hand for digging and backpacks on their shoulders for carrying off the jewels.

"Tell me again how we explain why we're taking shovels to a cemetery," Sloane said nervously.

"School archaeology project," Amelia said. "Though to be honest, I'm just sort of hoping the driver doesn't ask."

However, right about then, an all-too-familiar roar reached their ears as a motorcycle with a double sidecar screeched around South Park.

"Oh no." Amelia couldn't believe what she was seeing. "Is that . . ."

She couldn't finish the sentence. She just couldn't.

A bark finished it instead.

Bunny panted happily at them, his tongue lolling as he looked out from behind his goggles. Screeching to a halt, Belinda undid the chin strap on her own helmet and peeled it off.

"'Sup?" she asked.

"'Sup," Sloane managed faintly back. The best Amelia could do was give the scary librarian a little finger wave.

"You need a ride out to Principal Stuckey's farm?" Belinda narrowed her eyes at them both. "What's up with that?"

"Nothing's up with that." Sloane gasped, clutching her shovel like she might need to use it to fend off the librarian.

"Shouldn't you be at the library?" Amelia couldn't help but ask.

"Closes at three on Fridays. Then Bunny and I work as Uber drivers to make some extra cash. No one's ever gotten rich by being a librarian," Belinda chuckled.

True enough. But Amelia bet that lots of people had gotten rich by stealing someone else's stolen gems and then murdering them. Well, okay. Maybe not lots of people. Still, she was sure it had happened to someone, somewhere, sometime. And Amelia was *completely* confident that neither she nor Sloane wanted it to happen to them.

"What are you thinking?" Belinda asked them. "That the jewels are buried out there somewhere?"

"No!" Amelia and Sloane shouted together, startling Belinda and making Bunny whine anxiously.

"Then what's up with the shovels?" Belinda asked.

"We . . . saw a . . . tree out on the farm that, um, I wanted to give my dad as a gift," Sloane lied.

"What kind of tree?"

Amelia and Sloane exchanged a look. Sloane clearly didn't know what to say.

"The kind with leaves on them?" Amelia tried hopefully. "And, um, sticks?"

"And Principal Stuckey is cool with this?" Now Belinda was giving them the same look she'd given them that day she threw them out of the library. The one that made you think her eyes had actual laser beams hidden behind them. And she was thinking about singeing off your eyebrows and giving your hair a scary perm.

"You know what, you're right." Sloane grabbed Amelia by the shovel and dragged her back toward the porch. Amelia didn't put up any fight, deciding that retreat sounded like an excellent plan. "This is a terrible idea. What were we thinking?"

"Hey." Belinda's voice cracked through the air like a whip, catching them both just as they reached the porch steps and freezing them in place. "You still owe me for my time."

"Right, right." Amelia was glad that Sloane was brave enough to release her shovel and run forward to give Belinda a five-dollar bill. She practically threw it at the librarian before scurrying back to Amelia and the safety of the porch steps.

"You'll call me if you need to go anywhere?" Belinda asked menacingly. "Won't you?"

"Oh, definitely!" Amelia gasped, and then they both fled inside. Even though they heard the motorcycle take off again, they hid in the front parlor, peering out from behind the window curtains to make sure she'd really gone. Amelia could easily believe that the librarian had trained Bunny to drive the motorcycle and that she was slowly creeping up on the house to—to—to . . .

Honestly, Amelia didn't know. Bludgeon them to death with dictionaries? Slice them up with paper cuts?

"So much for Uber." Sloane shuddered. "Do you think *she* was the one who sent you the letters?"

"She's a definite possibility," Amelia said grimly. "Now what?"

"Now we call my grannies and hope they don't ask too many questions." Sloane pulled out her phone and FaceTimed them. However, rather than either Granny Kitty or Granny Pearl, Nanna Tia answered the call.

"Sloane-y!" The woman wore a different straw hat and flowered dress from the day before. She giggled at someone just off-camera and said, "Look, Timothy! It's our Little Sloane-y!"

Timothy? Wait, wasn't that . . .

"I know her!" Mr. Neikirk, the auctioneer, shoved his face into view. "She's one of the girls who've been working on figuring out where the missing Hoäl jewels have gotten to!"

"Did you know that I'm a Hoäl?" Nanna Tia asked him.

"Then you'll be filthy rich if they find those jewels!" Mr. Neikirk agreed happily, before chuckling, "Unless someone steals the stolen gems off of them, too, heh-heh-heh."

"What do you want, girls?" Sloane's great-grandma asked.

"Nothing!" Amelia and Sloane cried together. Then Sloane added, "Are, um, Granny Pearl and Granny Kitty there too?"

"Just making up some Jell-O salad! Want me to put them on?"

"Nope. Gotta go. Love ya, Nanna! Byeeee!" Sloane closed out of the app in a hurry.

"Sloane, he was at your nanna's house yesterday!" Amelia gasped. "And he wasn't playing bingo. He was just sitting there! He could be the one who set this all up!"

Grimly, Sloane said, "At least I know that if Granny Pearl and Granny Kitty are there, Nanna is safe. They can definitely take him."

"Your great-grandma is a local crime boss. I think she can take care of herself." Amelia looked anxiously at the time on her phone. It was still only four o'clock, and it wouldn't get dark out until after eight. That gave them about four hours to get there, dig up the graveyard, and get back without getting mugged, kidnapped, murdered, or some combination of all three. "Let me try Aiden or Ashley."

However, when she texted them, Amelia got this back from Aiden:

Principal Stuckey and Mr. Roth stopped by to talk to Mom and Dad. Something about abominable snowmen?

Oh, terrific. Amelia closed her eyes in pain. Now Aiden and Ashley would know too. She'd been sort of hoping that her mom and dad would keep the yeti business from them.

Only, hang on a moment. Wasn't it sort of weird for a principal and a teacher to make a house call over something like Amelia getting called names? Wasn't that the sort of thing that you phoned a parent about? And if you needed to speak to them in person, they came to the school? You didn't go to their house?

Unless you were trying to figure out what their child knew about some long-missing gems.

So you could steal them from their rightful heirs all over again.

Amelia explained the situation to Sloane, concluding, "My family won't work, either."

"There's nothing else we can do, then," Sloane said with a grimace. "We'll have to ride our bikes out there. You can ride one of my old ones."

Riding a bike was one more thing Amelia wasn't very good at. But doing something she was bad at was still better than hitching a ride with a possible murderer.

As Amelia and Sloane got onto their bikes to head out of town, they were quite right to be worried.

The person who had set this whole project in motion had been watching Amelia's YouTube videos with great interest.

That person now also knew they were on the move—and had a pretty good idea of where they were heading. Certain that whatever was left of the long-missing jewels was now within fingers' reach, this person picked up a slingshot.

And went to go join Sloane and Amelia.

16

BACK TO THE BEGINNING

With Amelia's short legs pedaling furiously on Sloane's old bike from when she was eight, it took the two of them close to an hour to make it out to Principal Stuckey's farm. Then they had to toss their bikes across the ditch and drag them through the soybean field that stretched between the road and the edge of the woods that had swallowed up the old cemetery. It was a bright day with plenty of hours of light left, but the leaves on the trees had gotten bigger and the shrubs on the ground thicker since they were out here last week.

The light coming through the branches was sort of purply green and the breeze made the iron sign that read SAUGLING CEMETERY creak in a way that Sloane refused to call creepy. It was . . . rusty. Yes, rusty.

Like nails in an old coffin.

Okay, she had to stop thinking thoughts like that. Clearly Amelia was not always a good influence on her imagination.

"Do you see the baby you were standing by when Mr. Roth gave us this assignment?" Amelia asked, looking around. The grass was already so high that it swallowed her up to the waist. As Sloane's eyes adjusted to the dimmer light, the graveyard began to look peaceful rather than sinister. There were lots of wildflowers, plus a bunch of squirrels and a family of bunnies hopping around.

"Um . . ." Sloane looked for the stone. There really weren't a ton of gravestones in the cemetery, but practically all of them were hidden by the weeds. "It was over by that big column that says 'Hoäl.'"

"You mean over by your great-great-great-great-grandparents' graves?" Amelia asked.

"When you put it that way, I kinda feel like I should have brought flowers or something, the way we do when we go to Mom's grave." Her mom would have loved all of this, Sloane thought. If she'd been alive, they wouldn't have had to ride their bikes out here. Maisy Osburn would have driven them here herself, shovel in hand.

Or maybe not.

Maybe she would have handed Sloane that shovel and said, *Go, have adventures with your friend Amelia. I'll be right here, waiting to hear all about them when you get home.*

She'd be happy that Sloane had finally found someone to have adventures with again.

"Here, we can bring them these." Amelia pointed at a clump of spring violets. She propped her phone up on one of the tombstones, leaned her shovel up against the tumble-down fencing, and yanked up a bunch.

Sloane lay down her shovel too, and together they set the flowers along the base of the Hoäl family marker and then looked around for the baby. It was easy enough to find. Running her fingertips through the grooves that formed the letters, Sloane was able to wipe away enough dirt to tell that the name beneath the statue of the baby definitely read "Lucy."

Her great-great-grandma.

Who had died too young of cancer. Just like her great-granddaughter would years later.

Sloane sort of wished she'd known about this graveyard sooner. Maybe her mom could have been buried here too. She would have liked that.

Just like Sloane, Amelia had been looking down solemnly at the ground. However, she must have been thinking very different thoughts. "You don't think he buried the jewelry *in* the coffin with her, do you?"

"Ugh. I hope not." Sloane made a face. "I'm not sure I want them badly enough to pick them off a dead person."

"Oh, I wouldn't mind, personally," a new-yet-familiar voice said. Sloane and Amelia whirled around.

To find Milton standing behind them.

"Looming menacingly over them" might be a better way to put it, actually. With a slingshot pulled back and aimed straight at them. He'd loaded an acorn into the pocket, and while Sloane didn't think it could kill them, she had no doubt that it would hurt quite a bit.

Meanwhile their shovels—which would have made handy weapons—were leaning against the fence back by the gate.

"Milton?" Sloane gasped. "But—but—you're Gryffindor!"

"Ha-ha-ha! That's exactly what a Slytherin would say if he wanted people to trust him!" Laughing maniacally, Milton dropped the slingshot long enough to yank off his glasses and toss them away into the weeds. He must have hit the family of bunnies, because they went flying in all directions. Before Sloane or Amelia could react, he had the slingshot pulled back again. "I don't even need glasses!"

"That Slytherin mug on your desk!" Sloane clapped a hand to her head, unable to believe she'd been so stupid. "The one you said your brother got you!"

"Ha! I don't actually have a brother."

"I even saw you drinking out of it!" Amelia dug her fingers down into her curls.

"I really wasn't sure I'd get anything out of this little plot of mine." Milton advanced slowly on them. "When I found out that Principal Stuckey lived on the old Zimmerman farm and invited the seventh grade out here every year, I knew that I could have over a hundred fresh young eyes looking for clues for me. When I ran into your teacher Mr. Roth at one of Timothy Neikirk's estate sales last winter, I realized I had the perfect dupe. I went all geeky on him, enthusing about what a great story the missing jewels were for a project! And he fell for it—hook, line, and sinker."

Milton laughed again, getting closer to them. Sloane and Amelia looked at each other out of the sides of their eyes and inched their way backward. There was no way he could get both of them with that slingshot. However, neither one of them wanted to do something panicky and desperate that might get the other one beaned on the head by that acorn. Like diving behind one of the half-sunken tombstones.

"Hey, stop moving!" Milton let the rock fly. It whizzed over the top of Amelia's curls and smashed against the Hoäl family marker, digging a small piece out of the marble. Before either one of them could do more than yelp, he'd reloaded. "That was a warning. Next time, someone's getting a goose egg on their forehead."

Sloane and Amelia exchanged a look and then reluctantly did as he said.

"You got pretty lucky that we discovered anything at all," Sloane pointed out, mostly to keep him talking. If she could get her phone out of her pocket without Milton noticing, she'd be able to FaceTime her grannies. If Milton knew that, maybe he'd run off without hurting her or Amelia.

Milton sneered at them, moving forward until he was right in front of them. "Like I thought any of you little twits were going to figure anything out! I just wanted you to find some new information but be too dumb to realize what any of it meant. I thought I'd have to spend another couple of years sorting through the clues to see where they pointed. Then suddenly you two were breaking into Ms. Popanz's office out at the spa and finding that secret compartment. Imagine my shock when it turned out to be empty. All that work for nothing! I couldn't believe my luck."

He sounded ridiculously bitter for someone who had let Sloane and Amelia do all of the work. Sloane slid her phone out of her pocket. However, she couldn't actually look at it without him noticing.

Then a glint sprang into his eyes, and he continued, "Except it wasn't exactly empty, was it?" Aiming the slingshot at Sloane, he added, "I saw you grab something out of there before anyone else realized it."

Once again, he sounded positively injured that she had done so.

Milton clearly saw himself as both the hero and the victim of this story. Sort of like Thomas and Jacob. And Charles and Oscar.

And right now, Sloane and Amelia.

However, Sloane did not plan on either one of them actually being a victim. Her thumb unlocked her phone, though she still couldn't risk looking at it without Milton noticing.

Amelia picked that moment to pipe up. "It was a note. From Jacob's son, Charles, to Thomas's son, Oscar."

"Amelia!" Sloane whispered through clenched teeth. *"Why are you talking to him?"*

"For the same reason you are," Amelia replied in a loud, clear voice that had to carry all the way across the cemetery to the squirrels sitting on the rickety fencing. "To keep Milton talking so he won't knock us out and steal the jewels *we* found. That *is* what you're planning on doing, right?"

"Well, I thought I'd knock you out, tie you up, and then steal the jewels. But yes, that's the general idea."

Sloane didn't like the sound of that at all. There were coyotes out here, and she wasn't certain that they wouldn't think two tied-up unconscious girls to be the perfect snack food. However, she realized why Amelia had been shouting rather than speaking in a normal voice. It wasn't panic; the other girl hadn't just set her phone on one of the tombstones.

She'd turned it on so it was recording everything.

That was a pretty good idea. If nothing else, if they got eaten by coyotes because of Milton, their murders wouldn't go unavenged. Forcing their ghosts to hang around this dumpy cemetery for the rest of eternity.

Ideally, however, Sloane would like to avoid being knocked out, tied up, and possibly eaten entirely. She was able to look at her phone long enough to pull up her recent calls. She tapped one randomly and hoped whoever she'd just called answered.

Meanwhile, to keep the museum curator talking, Sloane asked, "How did you find us?"

"Put a tracking app on her phone the other day when she was at the museum and ran outside to yell at you." Milton nodded at Amelia. "You really should password-protect your phone."

He giggled crazily.

"You've figured out where the jewels are, haven't you?" he continued. "They're somewhere in this cemetery."

"We'll never tell you where." Sloane clenched her fists.

"It's buried here," Amelia said.

"Amelia!"

"*What?*" Focusing her attention on Milton, Amelia continued, "It's here somewhere. You know that now, so you *could* try to knock us out with that slingshot. But you'll probably only get one of us."

"Ah, but which one?" Milton giggled again.

"Doesn't matter. One of us will get away."

"Possibly."

"Definitely." Amelia sounded very sure of herself. Looking down, Sloane saw that the other girl's fists were clenched too. "And then you'll only have a very little bit of time to dig up the jewels before the police arrive to carry you away."

"I can reload this slingshot *very* quickly," Milton warned.

"Yeah, but that still only means that you *might* get the jewels," Sloane cut in, hoping that whoever she'd called was listening to all of this. Whoever it was hadn't said a word, so she was praying that the call had gone through. "Or you could force us to dig up the jewels for you."

Turning her head slightly, Amelia gave her a little grin. Apparently, that was what the other girl had been trying to get him to do all along. Great minds thought alike.

"Trying to keep yourselves from being knocked out and tied up a little longer?" Milton laughed. "Doesn't matter to me if it's now or after you've tired yourselves out from all that digging."

"Later," Sloane said fervently.

"After we've tired ourselves out from digging," Amelia agreed.

Milton jerked his head toward the shovels. He kept the slingshot pointed at them as they clambered through the tall grass to get to their digging utensils.

"You've got until sundown," he said as Sloane grabbed her shovel by the handle.

"Oh, I think we've got longer than that." Amelia nodded at her phone. "I've been live-streaming us on YouTube ever since we arrived."

"*What?*" Horrified, Milton jerked his head over his shoulder.

Seizing the opportunity that gave them, Sloane leapt forward and used the metal bed of her shovel to knock the slingshot out of his hands. It disappeared into the thick weeds.

"NO!" The museum curator fell to his knees, scrabbling about in the grass for his lost weapon. However, Amelia dove forward and found it first, tossing it to the far side of the cemetery. Snarling, Milton pushed her away with so much force that she tumbled backward and hit her head on one of the stones.

"Amelia!" Whacking Milton out of the way with her shovel, Sloane ran over to her friend.

Who lay still.

Very, very still. With her eyes closed.

For one horrible second, the world went all shimmery for Sloane. Her legs wobbled too, quite certain that Amelia was dead.

Then the red-haired girl's eyes fluttered open and she put a hand to her head.

"Oooohhhh . . . my head hurts. Sloane, I think I have a concussion. I've never had a concussion before. Do people die of concussions?" Amelia gasped.

If Amelia could jump to the most dramatic conclusion possible, Sloane figured she was probably going to be okay. For the moment.

Then a stone tore a chunk off the top of the tombstone next to them.

"Drat!" Milton said from the other side of the cemetery. Of all the luck—the worst possible luck—he'd actually found his slingshot again.

"You stay here," Sloane told the still-woozy Amelia, propping her up behind one of the newer and less-wobbly-looking tombstones. The girl's head wasn't bleeding, but she clearly wasn't in any shape to run anywhere right now. That meant Sloane couldn't run off to get help, either, as Milton would have plenty of time to do something awful to Amelia if she did.

A wet, rotten acorn spattered onto Amelia's phone,

knocking it off the fence and sending the squirrels running in all directions. Sloane needed to pull Milton's attention away from her friend—fast.

"The police are probably already on their way, Milton!" Sloane shouted, daring to poke her head out around the side of the tombstone to see if Milton had moved any closer. Fortunately, hitting a target with a slingshot didn't seem to be the sort of thing Milton could easily do while running through an overgrown cemetery. He was still standing in the same place.

"Then I guess I'd better take care of you two before they get here!"

"Or you could grab the jewels and run."

"That's my plan. Once I've taken care of you two." Milton lifted up the slingshot again. Sloane dove forward, moving quickly from tombstone to tombstone for protection.

She almost didn't move quickly enough. An acorn cracked against the stone where her head had been only a fraction of a second before. If it had gotten her, she'd definitely be seeing double right now—assuming it hadn't knocked her out entirely.

"Sloane! Sloane!" Amelia called from the scrubby weeds on the other side of the cemetery. "Have you been hit, Sloane? Are you dying? It would be terribly tragic if we died together!"

"You're not dying, Amelia!" Sloane risked a peek around the edge of the stone.

She'd picked the wrong time to look. An acorn clipped her ear. Clapping a hand to the side of her head, Sloane jerked back behind the gravestone.

"She *might* be dying," the voice of their attacker called cheerfully. "You won't know unless you come out to see!"

"Don't do it!" Amelia cried woozily (but still dramatically). "I shall sacrifice myself nobly! Don't worry about me, Sloane! Save the long-lost Cursed Hoäl Treasure!"

Rolling her eyes, Sloane touched her ear. It stung but was only bleeding a little bit. Better still, Milton was focused on her now, not the injured Amelia. Sloane tried one last time to reason with the museum curator. "If you just let us go, you'll definitely have time to dig up the jewels."

Before Milton could answer, something rustled in the bushes behind him. As he turned to see what it was, Bunny leapt through a broken spot in the fencing and barreled into him with a ferocious growl.

The German shepherd knocked Milton to the ground with a thump of his paws against the museum curator's chest. He tore the slingshot out of Milton's hand with his teeth before sitting down on Milton. When the museum curator tried to get up, Bunny growled around the slingshot. Milton had the good sense to freeze meekly in place.

A second later, Belinda vaulted over the fence and into the cemetery too.

"You should be ashamed of yourself," she told Milton with a growl every bit as scary as her dog's. "Using your research skills for evil instead of good."

With that, she pulled a roll of bookbinding tape out of her jacket and used it to tie him up.

As Sloane opened her mouth to thank the librarian, she found herself yanked up off the ground.

"Sloane-y!" All of her various grannies cried, enveloping her in a hug. Then her dad was hugging her too.

"Amelia!" Various Miller-Poes swept into the cemetery to help Amelia to her feet.

"Does she need CPR? I think she needs CPR!" Aiden cried.

"No, no—she's having a panic attack!" Ashley insisted. "Does anyone have a paper bag or an oxygen tank?"

"She's been shot!" the Judge announced. "We need a tourniquet and a couple of bags of O-negative blood."

"Oh, don't be ridiculous, all of you!" Amanda Miller-Poe snapped. Turning to her daughter, she asked, "Amelia, can *you* tell us what's wrong?"

"Absolutely nothing," Amelia replied and pulled her family in for a group hug.

"Heh-heh-heh. Should have known better than to take on those young missies," Mr. Neikirk cackled, poking at Milton with the toe of his shoe. On the other side of the cemetery, Mr. Roth and Principal Stuckey hurried forward with the police hot on their heels.

"Those jewels should be mine," Milton whined as Bunny finally got off his chest and went over to where his person was standing with her arms crossed and a scowl on her face. "I'm the one who discovered that they were still missing! Everyone else had forgotten about them! They don't care about history! I do!"

"To think I invited you into my classroom!" Mr. Roth glared at the museum curator. "I trusted you!"

Belinda thrust her face into Milton's, the look on it frightening even this would-be cold-blooded thief. Slowly, threateningly, she said, "I thought you cared about knowledge. I thought you were part of my crew. If you ever get out of prison, you do *not* want to find out what happens when you cross a biker librarian."

"She'll turn your hide into a book," Amelia said dreamily, definitely concussed.

"I don't even know where my hide is!" Milton gasped.

"Wherever it is, you probably like it there better than on a book," Sloane warned him.

After that, Milton let the police carry him off without any fuss. He seemed to prefer that to being left with Belinda.

"How did you guys find us?" Amelia asked everyone. Still rubbing at her head, she confessed to Sloane, "I wasn't really live-streaming—just recording. I said that hoping Milton would believe it was true and run away."

"It was an excellent plan, and definitely saved us from being eaten by coyotes," Sloane assured her, somewhat relieved to find out that the world hadn't watched her yelping and ducking in terror. Slayer Sloane had a reputation to maintain, especially now that half of the seventh grade might be out to get her. To everyone else, she asked, "Was it my call that alerted you guys?"

Granny Pearl and Granny Kitty nodded their heads simultaneously. "You got us. While we all drove here, Timothy and Nanna Tia called the police and Amelia's family."

"You figured out where the jewels are?" Mr. Roth asked. When everyone turned and looked at him, aghast, he said, "Oh, come on—admit it. You're all dying to find them too, aren't you?"

Everyone looked around sheepishly at one another. There was no denying that he was right.

They all went over to Lucy's grave and looked down at it. Some of the excitement immediately drained out of the group. No one particularly wanted to dig up an old coffin. It seemed gross and disrespectful. Even if there were valuable jewels inside.

Principal Stuckey said, "Er, who wants to dig first? Anyone?"

No one did. Even the Miller-Poes seemed uninterested in winning this particular digging competition. Just the thought of it was gruesome.

Hang on a second. . . .

"Don't you think it's weird that Great-great-great-Grandpa Hoäl would bury the jewels with his beloved daughter?" Sloane said. "And then tell his bitterest enemy to go dig her up? I mean, there's no way I'd want something like that to happen to my mom."

"Ugh, I don't even want to think about it." Granny Kitty flinched and gave Sloane a hug. Her dad looked positivity horrified at the thought of it.

"See, that's my point," Sloane told the group. "He never would have done it. The jewels can't possibly be buried with her."

"And yet, he hid them as a testament to his love for her—and as a way to force my great-grandpa Kerr to witness the destruction he'd wrought," Amelia rambled dreamily, still concussed. "He blamed both Oscar and those jewels for her death. And so, he would have buried them with her."

Or at the very least, close by. Sloane looked around. Thomas

Zimmerman had hidden the jewels from Jacob Hoäl in a hidden compartment. What if Charles had turned the tables and done the same to Oscar?

Find the baby, find the jewels.

Sloane's eyes landed on the sculpture of the baby on top of Lucy's tombstone.

"Charles had to have put in that big family monument," Sloane said aloud. "The one with his mom's name on one side and his dad's on the other. He designed all of this."

She reached forward and twisted the limestone statue of the baby all the way around. It resisted at first, not having been moved in around ninety years. But she kept pushing, and as stone ground against stone, it swiveled to the side.

Pushing open the side of the Hoäl family plinth.

Everyone gasped. However, before anyone could step forward to see what was inside, Belinda said, "Sloane and Amelia should look first. They've earned it."

The adults all nodded in agreement. Sloane and Amelia smiled at each other and then went to look inside. Actually, Amelia tried to move forward to look inside and almost fell over. Sloane took her by the arm and helped her over to the monument.

Bending over, they looked together.

It was filled with jewels.

The Cursed Hoäl Treasure.

Minus some of the jewels, of course, as they would later find out. Oscar had sold off a few pieces here and there, including the tiara that had once belonged to a Russian czarina. (Which was a shame, as Amelia had secretly been desperate to try that one on.)

No, the long-lost Hoäl jewels were no longer worth thirteen million dollars.

They were only worth about six million.

Bad luck that they had been missing for so long? Zemblanity that some of them had been sold off so long ago?

Or good luck that they'd finally been found?

And serendipity that Sloane and Amelia had done it together?

Epilogue

You could look at it that Sloane and Amelia had been lucky to find the jewels that their too-many-great-grandparents had hidden away so many years before.

That's probably how Jacob Hoäl or Thomas Zimmerman or Charles Hoäl or Oscar Kerr would have looked at it. Actually, all four of them thought that they were entitled to the gems. Jacob because it was his money that bought them. Thomas because he was certain that he'd invested in Jacob's company. Charles because he should have inherited them from his father. Oscar because he *did* inherit them from his father.

Serendipity had most definitely played a part in Sloane and Amelia finding the jewels. However, had either one of them not bothered to talk, listen, and learn, zemblanity might have kept them apart instead.

Good luck and bad luck can play all sorts of terrible mischief with everyone's lives. Nothing can be done about that. But our choices matter too. It's the things we can control that lead to the greatest treasures. Like finding a new best friend. Or a hoard of long-lost jewels.

Neither Jacob, Thomas, Charles, nor Oscar ever really learned that lesson.

But their descendants Sloane and Amelia did. They knew it was wasn't luck that mattered the most.

It's how you choose to live your life around that luck.

In Sloane and Amelia's case, they chose to get some ice cream at Tiny's Dairy Barn, along with their families and friends. Then they were interviewed on the news.

National news this time, not just local.

Amelia was in heaven. Sloane was not.

However, the next night was Saturday night and everyone had finally left them alone by then. They were both happy, eating cheeseburgers and drinking milkshakes (also from Tiny's Dairy Barn). It was only open during warm-weather months, so the burgers in their old-fashioned wax paper always tasted to Sloane like summer vacation.

They were eating them together on the sparkling white floor of the Miller-Poe home theater in the sparkling white basement of the Miller-Poe house. Amanda Poe had winced at the sight of the burgers in their greasy wax paper but bit her lip and hustled upstairs without ordering them to eat outside.

"She's trying to make some changes," Amelia explained. "My whole family is. Tomorrow night is no longer Miller-Poe Tennis Night. It's Miller-Poe Silent and Classic Movie Night."

"I'm glad to hear it." Sloane smiled at her friend and slurped on her hot-fudge-and-marshmallow milkshake. Her Dad was at his Northwest Ohio Orthodontist Association banquet at the Barn Restaurant over in Archbold. With Cynthia Seife. And Sloane was okay with that.

Not great. But okay.

Nanna Tia was also out to dinner, but not at any orthodontist banquet. Mr. Neikirk was taking her out for dinner at Sullivan's Restaurant in downtown Wauseon to celebrate the fact that she was now a millionaire. Or at least would be, once the jewels were sold.

Of course, he was hoping she'd have him sell the famed Hoäl jewels for her. He was also head over heels in love with her.

"What a gal," he'd sighed dreamily to Amelia as they left the cemetery the night before. "Have you seen the way she runs that bingo game with an iron fist? She's like a very scary angel."

A very rich scary angel. Who had agreed to fund Amelia's very own film studio.

With Sloane's help, Nanna Tia was also going to fund the Maisy Osburn Bullying Prevention Program at Wauseon Middle School. Once the jewels were actually sold, Nanna Tia planned on giving rewards to Belinda, Bunny, Mr. Roth, and Principal Stuckey for coming to save Sloane and Amelia. The two of them had sort of hoped that Mr. Roth would release them from doing the rest of the project, but he said they still had to write their three-page paper.

At least he said their interview with CNN could count as both their presentation and their visual aid.

All around, life wasn't just okay. It was pretty terrific.

Tonight, Amelia and Sloane were going to watch the old home movies from the box Mr. Neikirk had sold Amelia. Sloane had brought along her goose, though she'd traded out the *Doctor Who* costume for the Queen Elizabeth costume. She sort of thought she'd keep the goose for herself. Nanna Tia planned on giving a big chunk of her money to both Granny Pearl and Granny Kitty, so they'd have more than enough money to buy their own fancy lawn ornaments from Norma.

When Amelia finally got the projector to work, she settled down on the floor next to Sloane. Together, they ate their burgers and drank their milkshakes while they watched the film.

Rather than someone's black-and-white home movies from the 1930s, the way they had been expecting, it turned out to be an old newsreel.

About a daring daylight bank robbery that had happened in downtown Wauseon back in the 1950s.

"I didn't know anything like that ever happened," Sloane said.

But Amelia didn't answer her.

Instead, the other girl had set down both her burger and her milkshake. She stood up slowly, hands clasped together.

Sloane wasn't at all sure she liked the look on Amelia's face.

"Uh, Amelia?"

"I bet it's never been solved!" Amelia gasped. "It's a crime that has gone unpunished for many moons! An injustice that needs to be righted! The scales of justice are out of alignment, Sloane! We must heed the cries of those who have been wronged!"

"Amelia, you can't mean . . ."

"I do mean it, Sloane."

Sloane slapped a hand to her face.

Amelia kept on dreamily, "We need to find out who did this."

"It's been more than seventy years!"

"That's sixty less than the last case we solved."

"We're not detectives, Amelia."

"But we could be, Sloane." Amelia smiled and spread out her arms. "Osburn and Miller-Poe Investigations and Film."

"That's not a thing!"

"But it could be," Amelia said again.

This time, Sloane didn't correct her.

Because she was right.

It could be.

Afterword

Wauseon, Ohio, is a real town with a real public library and a real creepy historical museum that was once a creepy school before becoming a creepy hospital and then a creepy apartment building. In seventh grade, I also did a real outdoor education day at our superintendent's farm and woods, where we learned about science, nature, and local history. Tiny's Dairy Barn, Sullivan's, and the Barn are all real places as well.

Alas, neither the Hoäl mansion nor the missing jewels are real, though the mansion was based on a real mansion in town with real secret compartments. Unfortunately, it was torn down a long time before I was born, which annoyed me greatly as a child. I was certain there had to have been treasure hidden in there somewhere, if only I'd gotten the chance to look for it!

All of the characters in this book are fictional, though Mr. Roth was named after my sixth-grade teacher and Mrs. Lemons after my next-door neighbor. However, at various points in my life, I've certainly felt like both a Sloane and an Amelia. (And we have all tangled with a Mackenzie at some time or another!)

Acknowledgments

Putting together a book is long, hard work, and it couldn't possibly be done without the help of many people. This begins with my parents, who entertained me as a child with scandalous and exciting stories of Wauseon's past. I'd also like to give a big thank-you to my husband, Sean, and daughter, Abigail, for their patience and encouragement. My friend Sara Yaklin also deserves thanks for providing me with both coffee and enthusiasm for my work. Thank you to my wonderful agent, Hilary Harwell, for all of her support and advocacy, without which I would still be sniffling over this story, wondering why no one loves it. An additional thanks goes to Brenna Franzitta for the fine work she did with the copyedits. And finally, thank you to Kate Prosswimmer and her assistant, Nicole Fiorica. Kate's insightful, spot-on edits make this book what it is. Without all of them, *Tangled Up in Luck* would never have been. One might almost say it was serendipitous how all of the right people came together to make it happen!